P9-BAU-005

THE IROQUOIS TRAIL:
Dickon Among the Onondagas and Senecas

THE JOURNEY OF MASTER Richard Sherwood IN THE YEAR OF 1616 A.D.

The Iroquois Trail

Dickon Among the Onondagas and Senecas

by M. R. HARRINGTON

(JISKO'GO)

Illustrations by DON PERCEVAL

RUTGERS UNIVERSITY PRESS

New Brunswick   *New Jersey*

Copyright © 1965 by Rutgers, The State University
Published by Rutgers University Press

Library of Congress Catalogue Number: 64-8262

Printed in the United States of America
by Quinn & Boden Company, Inc., Rahway, N. J.

Also by M. R. Harrington:
THE INDIANS OF NEW JERSEY: Dickon Among the Lenapes

AUTHOR'S NOTE

When I had finished writing *The Indians of New Jersey: Dickon Among the Lenapes,* it struck me that Dickon might have more adventures among the Iroquois tribes who lived not far to the north.

The background would not be difficult, as I had a number of friends among the Iroquois people and had visited many of their villages as a young man—even taking part in their ceremonies, in one of which, among the Oneidas, I was given an official Turtle Clan name Jisko'go, meaning "Robin." Among the Senecas, my nickname was Hosaistugge'teh, which means "He Carries a Snake," and was given me because I wore a snakeskin hatband.

Also, the Dickon period was not too late for me to bring in those three remarkable people, Hiawatha, Deganawida, and Jigonsasay, who founded the famous Five Nations League of the Iroquois, which, at the height of its power, practically put an end to warfare among the tribes of the northeast quarter of North America. And, of course, I could use their one-time enemy—Tadoda'ho, the fantastic Onondaga chief. So it was not hard to dream up *The Iroquois Trail: Dickon Among the Onondagas and Senecas.*

M. R. HARRINGTON
1964

CONTENTS

THE IROQUOIS TRAIL:
Dickon Among the Onondagas and Senecas

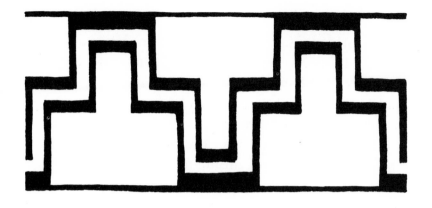

I. JAMESTOWN AND POCAHONTAS

The ship from England! Lord knows they were few enough in those days. When such a vessel cast anchor in the James River, the whole town gathered on the shore.

And in those days "James Towne," as they wrote it then, was only nine years old, and had seen some very hard times; but now, at last, it had begun to find a foothold. It was like a little walled city, only the walls were of wood, not stone. Triangular in shape with one broad side toward the river, it had projecting towers or bastions on all three corners. There were mounted cannons, commanding a full view of the outside of the walls and a well-guarded gate on the river side. If I remember, there were only twenty or thirty buildings in the village, ranging from huts to quite decent houses, but mostly simple cabins; also a church, a town hall and a jail.

And I—even I, who had so little in common with the

3

people of Jamestown, I too often joined the crowd. I watched the boats come in from the ships and the voyagers land—men, and sometimes even women, fresh from the land where I was born; the land which now seemed so distant and so foreign to me.

Sometimes, when I had a deer or other game to sell, I would paddle out to the ship in my canoe or Indian boat, which was dug from a log. My business would give me excuse to climb aboard, and look about. I loved it, and the smell of tarry ropes was as pleasing to me as the perfume of sweetgrass.

But when the *Dover Castle* came in on the tide that spring day in 1616—several days before she was expected, by the way—I watched her anchor splash into the river with a heavy heart. I knew the only real friends I had in His Majesty's new colony of Virginia were taking passage upon her—Matoaka, better known as Pocahontas, her husband, Mr. John Rolfe and their little son Tommy.

I did not have any blood kin in Jamestown, except my uncle, since my parents returned to England nearly a year ago. And the less said about my uncle, the better. I could not stand him. He was a man full of idle talk, who spent most of his life in the public house or tavern, drinking and gambling the hours away. The third son of the family he had always been a ne'er-do-well. For that reason, I learned, he had been shipped off to America to get rid of him, with a small stipend per year to live upon.

The first son of the family, the heir, had died without offspring before he could take over his inheritance. My father, as second son, had therefore returned to England with my mother, to straighten out the estate.

I had begged to remain in America, because, Indian-like, I preferred the freedom of river and forest to hunt and fish as I pleased and sell the products in Jamestown. But that was before I really knew my uncle, with whom I would have to live.

He did not like me any better than I liked him. He thought I was an uncouth lout in deerskin; a fool who loved to dress like an Indian and hunt game with bow and arrows. "No better than any cursed savage" were the words he often used to describe me. A special bone of contention between us was my dog Moonhakee. My uncle hated dogs, and his intention to kill the faithful little friend I had brought from the Lenape (Leh-nah'-peh) village became the cause of my leaving his roof.

Four years before that, as a boy of fourteen, I had been washed overboard from a ship bound for James-town, and was thought to be lost, as I had believed the ship to be. But the Lenape Indians had rescued me and taken me to their village of Turtle-Town. I had learned their language, lived their life—danced, hunted and even worshipped with them. I was adopted as a real member of the tribe. I loved these people, most of them anyway, and left them after more than two years when I learned that my ship had not been wrecked as I had supposed. My father had survived and was living in Jamestown and my mother was expected to arrive any day from England.

Perhaps I had changed somewhat during my years with the Lenape tribe. Certainly I had little feeling of kinship with these English in Jamestown, who forever squabbled among themselves. There were also many who would rather range the country "looking for gold" when they knew there was no gold. And they would rather seize food from the poor Indians, than till their fields and raise their own provisions.

Some new arrivals, I think, really took me for an Indian. It amused me to stand solemnly on the quay with my bow in hand, quiver on back, my dog at my side, and listen to them as they passed. They thought I was a "savage" without knowledge of English. I confess I even squinted my eyes to aid the deception, so they would not notice the blue color. My hair, in those days, was very dark brown and long, and not too wavy; and my skin was tawny from the sun. Also, my breast was tattooed, the largest figure representing a turtle.

I was standing thus, down on the float, when the first boat from the *Dover Castle* splashed in, swinging alongside, and the passengers hastened to disembark. Among them was a girl whom I noticed especially for the pink and white of her skin and the golden yellow of her hair. As I watched, a bundle she was carrying slipped from her hand, and in trying to save it from the river she lost her balance and fell in herself. In an instant the tide, still running strong, swept her away from the float.

Trained to quick action among the Indians, I cast aside my bow and quiver, plunged into the water, the dog following. In a few strokes I caught up with her, and succeeded in keeping her nose above water and steering her toward shore, while Moonhakee, my dog, saved the bundle.

We landed in the mud at the edge of the salt grass, and I had the girl in her draggled finery standing on solid ground by the time the people from the quay reached us. She clung to my arm and that gave me courage to speak out and tell them boldly that I would see her to her destination, wherever it might be. It seemed strange to me that there was no one among them to claim her or even to greet her. An Indian boy who had been in the crowd brought me my bow and quiver. With the bundle the dog had salvaged under my left arm and the girl clinging to my right, we finally reached higher ground.

"Where do you wish to go?" I asked—the first words I had addressed to her.

"To the palace, sir," she answered, rolling her blue eyes at me. "The palace of the Princess Pocahontas."

"There are no palaces in America," I explained, as gently as I could. "I can take you to the Rolfes' home, if you like. I know Pocahontas, who is Mrs. Rolfe; she is a friend of mine. Might I ask what your business is?"

" 'Tis no secret," she replied. "I have been sent to be maid and companion to the Princess on her voyage to England. But if America breeds such men as you, sir, perhaps I shall miss the ship!" And she squeezed my arm a little harder. I was eighteen years old and a grown man, but this girl was the first person who had ever called me "sir."

I felt my heart pounding; for the moment I knew not what to say. And before I could find words, she continued:

"My name is Betsy Yarnall, sir. Might I ask your name?"

"Richard Sherwood, at your service, ma'am. My friends call me Dickon."

By this time we had reached the Rolfe house, which stood not far from the gate. I knocked and knocked, but there was no response. Water was trickling from our clothing, and now my companion was beginning to shiver. So I took her around back of the house to the kitchen, a small separate building, and here I found the Indian cook, a tubby, middle-aged woman, who could speak some English. She grasped the situation at once and chased me out. I went home and put on dry breechclout, leggings and moccasins, and dried out and brushed my hair as well as I could. When I returned Miss Yarnall was dressed in dry clothing considerably too big for her (the cook's best) and was sitting with her back to the fireplace, drying her hair.

Now I learned from the cook that the Rolfes, not expecting the ship so soon, were away at the Indian village, taking leave of Mrs. Rolfe's family. Just now the yellow-haired Betsy did not wish to go anywhere with me "until she could get her clothes from the ship."

That night in my uncle's cabin was the worst yet. I cooked supper—venison stew, beans, corn bread. It was ready at the usual time, but my uncle did not appear. I waited and waited; finally I gave up and sat down to eat. Before I had finished he lurched in, smelling strongly of drink.

"What do you mean, eating before me?" he growled.

"I got tired waiting."

"Next time you wait for me, understand?" I said nothing. When we had finished, I gathered up the scraps for Moonhakee as usual.

"What are you going to do with that?" he demanded.

"Give it to my dog, of course."

"I forbid you to give any more of our food to that miserable cur!" He snatched the plate from my hand, went to the fireplace. "Better not," he mumbled. "Too much smoke." Then he said, "I'll throw it into the river tomorrow!" And he put the plate on a shelf.

A pretty mess! Here I furnish all the meat from my hunting trips, do all the cooking and wash all the dishes, since my mother left. And now I can't even feed scraps to my dog. Or so my uncle thinks. After he went back to the public house I took down the dish and fed Moonhakee.

Late that night I heard my uncle come stumbling in. The dog must have slipped in with him, because next morning I was awakened by my pet's cries. My uncle was kicking him out, muttering "I'm going to kill that cur!"

Later on, after I had washed the dishes and the old devil had gone back to the public house, I started out with the intention of finding Miss Yarnall, and showing her the sights. I had not gone far when I met her, walking with a soldier, becomingly dressed again. I bowed and said "Good morning," but she never even noticed me and passed me by with her nose in the air! And I had rescued her from the river only yesterday. Oh, why had I ever left Turtle-Town and my Indian friends?

I went out the gate; Moonhakee followed, limping. Once down on the quay I saw a big dugout canoe approaching with six paddlers and a steersman. In it I could see Pocahontas and her husband, with their little son. As it drew near I noticed that the steersman was no

less a person than the father of Pocahontas, called "Powhatan" because he was chief of the Powhatan tribe, although his real name was Wahunsonacock.

Of course I hurried down to the float; the canoe pulled up alongside and the paddlers grabbed hold; I lent a hand to Pocahontas, who was carrying the child; then to Mr. Rolfe.

"What's the matter, Dickon?" he cried. "You look sick!"

"Something bad happen?" asked his wife.

"Oh, I am sick, sick at heart. Things are getting worse and worse for me here; nobody likes me except you two, and you're going away. I've told you how my uncle hates me; just this morning he said he's going to kill my dog. I feel like jumping into the river! I wish I'd never left Turtle-Town."

It was Pocahontas who spoke up.

"You better go back there—go back to your Lenape

friends. Stay there until your folks come back here."

"Oh, it's so far," I groaned. "And there's that big bay to cross—what you call the Chessa-peek. And my canoe is too small to fight the big waves."

Pocahontas talked with her father in their own language; finally she turned to me.

"My people will help you," she said. "They take you in big canoe away north to far end Chessa-peek—maybe seven, maybe eight days. Then you walk, not very far, 'bout one day east to Lenape River; then you go up river. Second day you find Turtle-Town!"

"Oh, that would be wonderful!" I cried. "But how can I pay them for such a long trip? I have nothing."

"No pay," she answered. "You my friend; my father, he's chief. That's enough!" She talked with her father again. "You come here, 'morrow morning, just getting light. You hide in bushes, down there, you see?" She pointed to a clump some two hundred paces down from the quay. "Wait until canoe come, take you and dog."

Then John Rolfe broke in.

"Better be careful," he said. "Get your things ready tonight before that precious uncle of yours comes home. Then when the time comes, sneak out without wakening him!"

I liked John Rolfe—a brisk, cheerful young man with a small reddish chin beard; he held an important position, too—Secretary and Recorder for the Governor of the Colony.

"And another thing," he warned, "if it's foggy, they will have a sentry patrolling the shore along here. If he sees a canoe, he might fire!"

Again there was a conference; then Pocahontas said, "If we got fog, you stay in bush until you hear shore-bird call 'twees-twees-twees;' then you answer with same call. If same call answer you again, come down to shore. Let's hear you make call!" I tried until I had it right; John was amused; even the Chief grinned.

"What if the soldier is near when I hear the call?" I asked.

"Oh that's bad!" Pocahontas said and relayed the question to her father, who, after a few words, made another call—"whoo-oo-oo-oo." Then she gave me the answer, "If soldier come, you make call like little owl, then canoe wait." I practiced that one, too.

"I can help you about another matter," John said after we finished the birdcalls. "I'll tell the gate keeper to let you out early to go hunting. I do not have to tell what you will be hunting for."

Well, the time had come. John Rolfe shook the Chief's hand, spoke to him in his own language; Pocahontas let her father caress little Tommy, his grandson; then sadly took her leave. I saw tears in her eyes. The canoe pulled out as we all watched and waved.

As we walked back into the village I told them of the maid who had arrived on the ship—but did not call her fickle. Then I said farewell with a sad heart, although I did not suspect that I would never see my friend Pocahontas again.

Pocahontas was already the wife of John Rolfe when I first met her; she came down to the quay with my parents when I arrived from Turtle-Town. A really beautiful woman she was, with large dark eyes, a straight nose, small mouth, full lips and a firm chin. Her smooth skin was lighter than that of most Indians, perhaps because, as an English housewife, she was not exposed so much to the sun. With our common interest in her race we became good friends; in fact it was she who persuaded my parents not to complain about my wearing Indian garb; although all three agreed that I should get rid of my Lenape warrior's crest haircut and scalp lock—which I did.

When I asked her one day the meaning of her name, she laughed.

"Everybody call me Pocahontas," she said. "But my real name Mataoka. When I was little girl I have fun, play all the time; that's how I get Pocahontas name; that means 'Playful One.' "

Her English was not perfect, yet easily understood and slowly improving. She could understand practically anything said to her in English; if not, she would ask, without hesitation, to have it explained.

If that woman ever did one wrong or wicked thing in all her life, I never heard of it. However, some Indians thought that she should not have saved the colony by bringing all that food to Jamestown when the people were starving; because the English wanted to take over the Indians' homeland which was wicked.

That night after supper, as soon as my uncle had left, I gathered all my Indian equipment and hid it behind the woodpile outside our cabin. Then I added two new hatchet heads and a good knife from my father's stock of supplies, wrapping them in a piece of buckskin. Naturally I slept very little; I slipped out when I saw the first gray light through the window panes—tiny diamond-shaped ones in those days.

It was so foggy I could hardly see where to go. I gathered my things; the gatekeeper let me out without trouble; Moonhakee followed. We were hardly settled in our bushy hiding place when I heard an ominous clanking tread—a sentry was passing! And a few minutes later I heard "twees-twees-twees" from out on the water. I answered, heard a reply—was starting down to the shore when—I heard the clank-clank again. The sentry was coming back. Panic-stricken I sounded the warning little-owl call. The clanking stopped. The sentry suspected something.

What could I do? I was trembling all over. Moonhakee cowered low. After a few minutes the sentry, hearing nothing more, walked on. I waited a bit, sounded the shore-bird call again, got a reply, hurried down to the water's edge. The canoe took form out of the fog, the bow grated on the beach. I helped Moonhakee in, put down my bundle, scrambled in myself. The paddlers pushed; in a moment we were safe—hidden in that gray cloud. But I was wet with sweat.

I saw that there were two men paddlers with one old woman steering; she was skinny and small, with hawklike face and bright black eyes. Her only garment was a short, wrap-around buckskin skirt, fringed at the bottom; her hair hung in one braid at the back. The paddlers were young men, one shorter and fatter than the other; their hair was long like mine. All they wore were little buckskin breechclouts.

They spoke no greeting, but Fatty beckoned me to

hand him my bundle and my bow and quiver, which he passed back to be added to a pile of baskets, bed mats and robes near where Grandma sat; then Lanky spread an old robe over the lot.

How they found their way down river I don't know; I could not see a thing; probably they just followed the current of the ebbing tide, watching out for rocks and snags. After a while a brisk west wind sprang up and scattered the fog. About midday they stopped paddling and drifted, while Grandma served us pieces of dried venison and little corn cakes, with water out of a big gourd bottle. Before sunset we had reached the great Chessa-peek bay, and landed for the night on the point north of the river's mouth.

As soon as we landed and pulled up the canoe, Grandma unpacked the sleeping mats and deerskin robes —I noticed there were four of each, which meant a set for me; also a number of baskets and bags. Meanwhile Fatty had started a fire with some fire sticks he carried in a small rawhide case, while Lanky gathered driftwood; before I knew it, Grandma was cooking our supper. It was really good—a stew of dried venison and hulled corn with a little bear's grease, also some fresh hot corn cakes, now called "corn pones." She cooked the stew in a pottery kettle which she had brought in one of her baskets, packed in grass; the pones she baked over hot coals on a piece of broken pot.

As my companions talked together I found I could understand a good part of what they said, because of the likeness of the Powhatan language to Lenape—and they could grasp much of my Lenape speech.

Next morning, after a good breakfast, we started to cross the Chessa-peek. But the waves were running so high from the west wind that my companions decided to turn back, and work our way north along the west side of the bay, where we could enjoy the shelter of the land.

I think it was the third night that we put in at an Indian village on a cove opening upon the bay. Here the Chief heard that I was a friend of Chief Wahunsonacock and his daughter Pocahontas, and that they had arranged this trip for me. Because of this, he put on a feast for us at the village council house, with fresh meat for a change, and dances with drum and rattle. Even Moonhakee was given a large chunk of fresh deer meat without bones. This stop gave Grandma a chance to fill her gourd water bottles at the village spring.

Before the trip was over, I was able to provide fresh meat several times from early morning hunts. And with my fishline and hooks I brought in considerable fresh fish which tasted better than the dry fish Grandma had provided; also I dug a few clams for us. In the evenings, after supper, we often amused ourselves singing Indian songs—they in Powhatan; I, naturally, in Lenape.

We passed what seemed to be a big side bay on the left, but they managed to explain that it was the mouth of a river called Potto-mak. Just before the trip ended we crossed the mouth of a large river from which muddy water flowed; they gave a form of the name Susquehanna, which means "Muddy River" in Lenape. I remembered, only too well, that it was the Susquehannock Indians, who live on this river, that attacked our Turtle-Town village at one time.

For some time the Chessa-peek had been getting more and more narrow. Finally, shortly after noon one day, we reached the end. The canoe grounded, my friends laid out all my things; Grandma fixed me a pouch of dried venison and one of parched corn, toasted and ground, to feed me on the rest of my journey. I opened my bundle and laid the two hatchet heads and the knife some distance apart on the beach. Then I explained in Lenape:

"It is bad to give a friend anything with a sharp edge; but I hope you two men 'find' the hatchets after I am gone, and my girl-friend here, the knife." Then Grandma thought of something—I had no mantle or cloak; so she picked out the best of the buckskin robes we had been using, and hung it about my shoulders, and I thanked her in Lenape. And finally Fatty said something in Powhatan about two trails, one straight east to Lenape River (doubtless the one Pocahontas had mentioned) and another (he pointed northeast) longer, but coming out nearer to Turtle-Town.

I picked up my things and departed, but before I entered the forest I turned and waved; they were picking up my offerings, but they saw me and waved back. I headed northeast on a plain trail; Moonhakee followed. He seemed quite excited; I wonder if he knew we were nearing home? Or perhaps he was simply glad to travel on land again.

That trip through the forest seemed endless; we spent two nights in the thickets; but late the next day I spied an opening ahead and in a short time we stood on the bank of the Lenape River, now called the Delaware. Moreover, it was a spot I knew well; there was a deep pool where, years ago, I had come sometimes to fish. I took out my fire sticks from my arrow quiver, made a little blaze, threw on some tobacco, and gave thanks to the Maker of All that we had arrived in safety. Twelve times I threw tobacco. The Lenapes believe that on the twelfth time the prayer reaches the Great Spirit.

II. TURTLE-TOWN AND WHITE-DEER

The dog and I started upstream along the west bank of the river. After a while, crossing a rise, we saw the bark roofs of Turtle-Town. When I saw them, I remembered something—my eagle feather. I had won it when I rescued Bowl-Woman and her baby from the Susquehannock raiders who had captured them. It was in a rawhide case attached to my quiver. I took it out, reached up and tied it to my hair in back. Then we began to pass gardens; in some of them green sprouts were already shooting up from the corn hills. Well I remembered how as a servant-captive I had helped the women dig small holes about four feet apart. In each hole a fish was laid; then we piled over it a little mound of earth in which we planted a few grains of corn.

In two of the gardens, although the sun was low, women were working. They stood and stared as we passed;

but they did not recognize me, nor I them. Approaching the village, I smelled woodsmoke; I heard dogs barking, people laughing and talking, children shouting and crying. I felt my heart pounding. Under the shed of the first bark-house we passed, lay a dog; he jumped up, rushed out at us barking; Moonhakee braced himself. But when they caught each other's scent they relaxed; their wagging tails told that they recognized each other; they were old friends. And well they might be; I had lived, and so had Moonhakee, in that house, the home of Cross-Woman, when I was nothing but a captive boy, her servant or slave.

Turtle-Town looked about the same; the square or rectangular houses covered with sheets of elm bark, some with gable roofs, some arched; a few scattered dome-shaped huts, thatched- or mat-covered, all the houses grouped around the village square, all facing east. The square itself opened east onto the river bank; in the middle stood a large bark-covered ceremonial building, the "Big-House," where I had been adopted.

I had many memories of that village, most of them pleasant. As a captive boy I had worked, not only in the gardens which furnished the vegetable food; but had helped the women make deerskin clothing, even pottery. And I had watched with interest how they made baskets, woven bed mats and bags of fiber and sewn roof mats of rushes; they also did beautiful embroidery with dyed deer hair or porcupine quills.

Later after being adopted I had done my share as a hunter, bringing in meat for my new family, and had learned how to make things of wood as the men did, from canoes down to spoons and the like; to shape tools of stone and make beads of shell. I had taken part in the ceremonies, earned my eagle feather as a young warrior at the time of the Susquehannock raid.

We crossed the square, heading for the home of Thunder-Arrow and Bowl-Woman, the couple who had adopted me; or rather, Bowl-Woman had, with her husband's agreement, for only women have that privilege.

The house, which I had helped to build after the old one had been burned by the Susquehannocks, looked about the same; but some things seemed wrong. There were no bundles of arrow-making switches such as Thunder-Arrow always had hanging under the shed—and no venison on the meat rack, although there were still strings of corn. Wondering, I stepped into the house.

The inside looked much as I had remembered it; the small fire pit in the middle; the smoke hole overhead, the sleeping platform, neatly built of poles, about a yard wide and two feet off the ground, with three sides against the wall. In the back, where Bowl-Woman and Thunder-Arrow slept, the supporting posts had been run about four feet higher, to carry another platform; but nobody slept up there; it was used for storing precious things.

There was my mother, Bowl-Woman, preparing to set a cooking pot on the fire; a small boy was playing with corncobs on the floor. White-Deer, once my sweetheart but now my brother's wife, was sitting on the edge of a sleeping platform, nursing a baby. But Thunder-Arrow, my father, was not to be seen; neither was my brother, Little-Bear.

I said, "Mother!" in a low voice.

Bowl-Woman heard me, rose quickly to her feet, stared at me in the dim light, her mouth open. "Can it be—are you—In-The-Forest?" she gasped. I nodded. The next minute we were in each other's arms. "Oh," she sobbed. "I didn't know you—you have grown so tall—your hair is long again; but I see you still have your eagle feather." The tears were trickling down her face. She was a rather short, good-looking woman with big kindly brown eyes; but I could see that she was aging.

"I am thankful to be back with you," I managed to say.

Somebody nudged me. There stood White-Deer who had laid the baby down on the sleeping platform.

"Don't I get just a little squeeze too?" she asked. "After all I am your sister." I threw one arm around her. She was really pretty in the Indian way, with fine smooth skin, round face, large eyes a little slanted, long lashes, a small curved nose and a very small mouth.

How long we would have stood there I don't know, but we heard Moonhakee whining. He had gone under the platform where he used to have his bed, a nice, soft, old fur robe, but it was gone. Bowl-Woman patted his head. "We are glad to see you back, too," she said. "I'll fix a bed for you." And she did.

I looked about; there was no trace of Thunder-Arrow's tools, supplies, unfinished arrows, even clothing. Crippled by an old battle wound, he had been unable to hunt, but supplied his family with meat and skins by making arrows and trading them to the hunters.

"Where is Father?" I asked.

Bowl-Woman could not speak at first. Then she murmured, "Didn't you know? He died seven moons ago. Roaring-Wings doctored him, tried to save him, but it was no use; we think it was that old wound that killed him."

"And that's not all," White-Deer said. "My husband is gone, too. About four moons now. He has never seen his little son, White-Tooth."

"Why, I thought he must be out hunting. What happened?"

"Men-gwee warriors carried him off, for a hostage, they said. But they are cruel people; we think they must have killed him or he would have come back to us."

I knew that "Men-gwee" meant the fierce Long-House people who live in the north, now called Iroquois. It sounded bad.

"Now you know," said Bowl-Woman, "why we have no meat to offer you tonight, only *sup-pan* hominy. And I know you must be hungry. We never have meat any more, or even bear's grease, unless somebody gives us a present. We women do not mind it so much, but your little brother here," she pointed to the boy on the floor, "needs it to grow on."

"I would not know him, he has grown so big," I said. "The last time I saw It-Is-Approaching he was still on the cradleboard." Then I added, "Tomorrow I hope to bring in a deer. In the meantime take these." And I handed her the sacks the Powhatan woman had given me. There was still some dried venison in one, toasted parched corn meal in the other.

Bowl-Woman heated the *sup-pan* in the pot and we ate a frugal supper. Then she spread a sleeping mat on my old bed-platform, handed me out two skin bedcovers or robes which I recognized as my old ones. She had kept them, apparently unused, all this time. And I noticed that White-Deer was sleeping on the big bearskin I had left word should be given her after I had gone.

And so I took up the old life: I kept my family supplied with venison, even traded two deer for a sack of bear's grease; I looked up old friends who were still alive, as most of them were. All seemed glad to see me.

Yes, I took up the old life—as nearly as I could, but I was far from happy. When my old friends planned to give a feast to celebrate my return, I told them, "No." I just did not have the heart.

My adopted father, Thunder-Arrow, was gone forever, and I had looked forward to his companionship, his instruction and his joking. My best friend, and adopted brother, Little-Bear, was gone, and I could not help worrying about him. But my greatest present problem, strange to say, concerned White-Deer, my brother's wife.

Her eyes were ever upon me when I was near. She went out of her way to do special things for me. And every time I came in from the hunt she embraced me fondly, a thing Indian people seldom do, except to greet old friends or relatives who have been long absent.

Certainly I could not bear to tell her not to do this. In truth I felt strongly drawn to her—which was to be expected. She had been my boyhood sweetheart, and had married Little-Bear only when I told her I was too young to marry, which was the truth at that time. And Bowl-Woman watched all this with an approving eye.

They could not be blamed. They thought Little-Bear dead, while I, deep down inside, felt that he was still alive and might return to his wife and child someday. And so I fought off my feeling for White-Deer, fought it off, fought it off.

The crisis came one day while I was passing the house of Fling-Her-This-Way, White-Deer's mother. She was at the door, saw me, beckoned me in. She was a tired-looking, worn little woman. She had been a widow for many years, who had lived and raised her daughter on the products of her garden and gifts, now and then, of pieces of venison from her brother. Now she said to me:

"My daughter has asked me to tell you something that she cannot say herself. She loves you very much, and she feels that you love her. With her husband dead, she is free and now she wishes to become your wife."

I managed to stammer something about not knowing whether Little-Bear was dead or not and how awful it would be if he returned and found me, his brother and best friend, married to his wife. One thing sure, I had escaped from one bad situation at Jamestown only to encounter a worse one here.

What could I do? I was really getting desperate. Then I remember that, as a boy, I had gone to the old doctor, Roaring-Wings, for advice. He was a real friend; I had given him the first deer I ever killed, and he had held a little ceremony at that time and prayed that I should always have good luck in hunting. He was a short stout man with long gray hair and a square jaw. Strange to say, his wife was taller than he, withered and thin, but her hair was still quite black. They were sitting on their sleeping platform, talking together, when I came in.

Now he welcomed me, and patiently listened to my story, raked out some hot coals, burned some tobacco, prayed for guidance in a low voice. Finally he said, "There is only one right thing to do and that is a hard one. You must find out whether your brother is still alive. Then, if he is, get him released so that he can come back to his family. If you find proof of his death, then you return and take White-Deer to be your wife. Now there is one thing more: if he lives and returns here, it will be best if you do not come back. I am sorry to tell you this, but I am sure I am right."

"But why?"

"You might be able to hold in your own feeling, but with White-Deer's feelings toward you, as you have told it, there would surely be family trouble. There is one other thing you could do, if what I said seems too hard."

"What is that?"

"Just go away and stay away—try to forget the whole thing."

"That I could not do," I told him. "Tell me, just what happened when the Men-gwee-uk took Little-Bear? Then I shall know better what to expect."

"A strong party of their warriors came here with a man who could speak their language and ours. They asked for a council to be called, and when this was done their leader said they were trying to keep the tribes from fighting among themselves. And they, the Men-gwee-uk, wanted us, the Lenapes, to be their chief peacemaker. First, we were to promise not to go on the warpath any more. Second, if anyone attacked us, we were to call upon the Men-gwee-uk for help. And third and most important, we would try our best to persuade other tribes not to fight each other; if they persisted we should tell them the powerful Men-gwee-uk would come and punish them; if they still refused our advice, we should send a messenger to the Men-gwee-uk, who would then come and destroy them if necessary. Most of our council, after it had been talked over, agreed; but there were two who said that this would turn our warriors into women, that it would 'put skirts' on all of us. And because these two objected, the Men-gwee-uk took Little-Bear as a hostage, promising to care for him well if we kept our agreement; but threatening to kill him if we did not. And the same thing took place in other Lenape villages, although in some of them, I have heard, when the full council agreed, no hostages were taken. We have kept our promise, so Little-Bear may be still alive."

"I have thought that he is, all along," I said. "But tell me, with this agreement, can't we even fight off the Susquehannocks if they attack us again?"

"Oh yes, of course we can defend ourselves; then we report the attack to the Men-gwee-uk, and they, not we, will send a party to punish the Susquehannocks."

"What gave the Men-gwee-uk that notion? Did they say?" I asked.

"Yes," my friend replied. "Their leader explained it. It seems that there in the north are those five Men-gwee tribes, living side by side, who speak languages somewhat alike. They decided to get together, and not fight each other any more, and to join forces if any outside tribe attacked them. It worked so well that now they have planned to urge other tribes to stop fighting, and if they won't stop, to compel them. And with their five tribes joined together they have the power to do it."

"It's a good thing I won my eagle feather when I did!" I said. "Now tell me, how do you think I should go about this task?"

"Go up into the Men-gwee country; make friends with them; travel from one village to another. In time you should find Little-Bear, or learn that he is no longer living. If you find him, then comes the question of getting him released; that you will have to work out."

"But they talk a different language!"

"There must be, here and there, someone who can speak both tongues. They have captured some of our people in the past, and, I have heard it said, adopted them.

But be careful, do not anger the Men-gwee-uk. They might kill you!"

"How can I get to the Men-gwee country?" I asked.

"I have never been there, but this is what the Men-gwee leader said when he told us to send a messenger to report fighting. Almost north, you follow the Lenape River, until you reach the place where it makes a bend, comes in from the east. Here leave the river after maybe nine or ten days travel and go northwest. He said there is a plain trail, and in about two days more you will reach the country of the Onondaga tribe, the middle one of the five Men-gwee nations."

"I shall try it," I said, "and only hope I succeed. There is one thing I wish you could do for me; if you agree it will give me more courage, keep me from worry. Try to get the hunters of this village to give a piece of meat now and then to Bowl-Woman and White-Deer. The women say they can get along with just corn and beans and dried pumpkin, but my little brother needs meat to grow on."

At that point Roaring-Wings' wife, who had been listening, spoke up. "They should be willing to do it, too. Little-Bear is a hostage for the whole village after all. His family should not go without food."

"I promise," said Roaring-Wings. "And I shall pray for you; that you may be safe and that all may turn out well. And one more thing. I heard you gave your hunting charm to Little-Bear. I have another right here."

I took it and thanked him. It was a tiny wooden mask, painted half black and half red, made to represent *Mee-sing-haw-lee'-kun,* the Guardian of Game. It had a neck thong so the hunter could wear it on his breast. And I put it on.

When I reached the house, White-Deer threw her arms about me. My arms crept around her waist. The poor girl did not know what was going to happen, and I did not speak of it that night. But next morning, after we had eaten, I told them frankly that I was going to leave, as soon as I could get ready; and explained the plan to them.

White-Deer was silent for a while. Finally she said, "You are a brave man and it may be that you are doing right." She looked at the baby, saw that he was asleep on his cradleboard, picked up a robe, threw it over her head. "I just can't stand it to watch you go. But I shall be waiting." She went out the door. I looked out; she was headed for the forest. I felt sick at heart.

But Bowl-Woman thought the scheme was wonderful, but dangerous. Because she was his mother, it was natural for her to approve any plan to find and rescue Little-Bear. I did not dare tell her of Roaring-Wings' warning—not to return to Turtle-Town myself if the plan succeeded.

Now she hurried around and fixed me a shoulder-bag of *ka-ha-ma'-kun,* parched corn toasted and ground, like the Powhatan women had given me; but this tasted better, because it was mixed with tree sugar, now called maple sugar. Also, of course, she filled a woven bag of dried venison for me. She had dried the meat of some of the deer I had killed.

Then she said, "If you are going up the river, why not take our canoe? It is lying up on the river bank, where it has been all winter, covered with mats. There is nobody in the family now who can use it, except you."

I had to explain to her that on account of the rapids and the swifter current I would find up river, I could make faster progress by walking. I put on my shoulder pouches, hung my quiver on my back. It was too much for her, she took me in her arms again, weeping silently. I picked up my little brother, embraced him, took up my bow and called Moonhakee, who left his comfortable bed with reluctance. Then we set forth. I did not say farewell to my old friends, I simply could not stand it. Besides, the less said and known about this trip the better.

It was a long and weary journey up that river, now called the Delaware. I lost count of the days, maybe it was eight, nine or ten. Following the west bank, we traveled first northeast, then northwest, then passed the rapids. Later on we crossed a large branch coming from the west. The country was becoming rough, with quite high mountains; in one place the river came through a sort of gateway between them. We passed a number of villages; the people I talked to spoke the Lenape language a little differently; they belonged to the Min'-see tribe of the Lenape, while Turtle-Town was U-na'-mee.

We lived mainly on dried venison and *ka-ha-ma'-kun,* although I did kill a few rabbits and a turkey, so Moonhakee and I could enjoy a little fresh meat. But I did not hunt deer, because most of it would be wasted. In one Min'-see village we were invited into the home of the chief, and enjoyed a real meal with *sup-pan* and fresh corn cakes, which Moonhakee shared. I kept away from villages as much as I could to avoid questioning as to the purpose of my journey.

At last we reached that bend in the river, where it came from the east. And here, after some search, I found a trail leading northwest—this we followed.

III. THE GIRL WITH SHORT HAIR

It was hot and muggy, that fateful day, with ominous distant rumbles of thunder in the west as we trudged, my dog and I, through the seemingly endless forest. Would we never reach the Men-gwee villages? Suddenly Moonhakee stopped, ears erect. I listened— now I could hear it too, the faint yap-yapping of dogs. As I stood, my nostrils caught the scent of woodsmoke. Some sort of human habitation must be near. Could it be an Iroquois settlement?

But the sound came from the left—not the direction of the dim trail that I was following. I glanced about. A steep bluff, marking the edge of the valley, loomed through the trees to the right. Perhaps, if I climbed up there, I could see something.

See detailed double-page map at the center of the book. Each village, river, and lake is located, and Dickon's journey can be followed easily by the reader.

Unfortunately for me, as it turned out, Moonhakee did not come along. He had found a mouse hole or something, and the last I saw of him he was digging busily. He might have scented danger and warned me, had he followed me up that hill. Reaching the top, I looked toward the west over the valley.

Sure enough, there it was, the largest Indian town I had ever seen; a huddle of rough roofs, some rounded like loaves of bread from my mother's oven in England. There seemed to be more than a hundred houses, with the creek beyond. The houses were fenced in, held like sheep in a giant pen by upended tree trunks forming a great palisade which made this town a fortress. Beyond the log walls the lush green cornfields spoke of peace, peace and plenty. Yet I knew this town would be a nest of hornets if annoyed. Those bark roofs below me were large, and too long for the Indian lodges I knew; they must belong to the Long-House Builders, the dreaded Iroquois, called Men-gwee-uk by the Lenapes.

But though the dread lay deep in my heart, this was the town that I had traveled so far to see. The hard journey north through the hills and forests was ended; now came the task of making friends with this strange people. Somewhere, in one of their many villages, my adopted brother, Little-Bear, was held hostage, and he must be found.

I was standing there, planning my next step, when someone grabbed my hair from behind and jerked me over backward. Swarming warriors, appearing from nowhere, seized me. I struggled frantically, but in a few seconds found myself helpless. When my brain cleared,

I was looking up into a hideous face, little more than a skull covered with yellow skin and framed in many snaky braids of hair. The sunken eyes glittered evilly; the thin lips were twisted into a fiendish grin.

Now I heard growls, shouts, blows; then a dog howling in pain. It was Moonhakee's voice; the poor fellow, I thought, had discovered my plight and tried to rescue me; but they had driven him off, perhaps killed him.

It took but a moment for the warriors to strip me

of weapons, shoulder pouches, clothing. They tied my
hands tight together and fastened a rope about my neck.
Then they dragged me down the hill toward the town.
Outside the palisades they halted and talked together in
their strange language, of which I could not understand
a word. It was not at all like the Lenape tongue, which
I knew well.

I looked at the monster who had captured me as he
stood talking with his men. I had just about made up my

mind he was human after all, just a villainous old man and not a fiend, when my blood chilled again. I saw one of his many hair braids, hanging loose around his shoulders, raise itself and writhe up to the top of his head. It was a live snake. Was the creature a demon with snakes growing out of his head like hair? As I looked closer even his body and arms seemed snaky, all tattooed with little diamond figures in rows.

They dragged me to a gateway in the palisades, and here they freed my hands and gave me a gourd rattle, making signs I should shake it. And so we marched into town, my captor at the head of the procession. I was led by the neck like a beast to the slaughter, shaking the rattle as I walked. Armed warriors with arrows on the string surrounded me, ready to shoot if I tried to escape.

My memories are so confused I hardly know what took place. But I can say that they pulled me up on a low scaffold or platform in the middle of the public square. And when they had finished, I was tied to an upright square frame of poles with my arms and legs stretched out to the four corners, not knowing what frightful end was planned for me.

Then my wrists began to pain horribly and my arms and legs to ache, worse and worse—the sun beat down hotter and hotter. Somewhere I had heard that a warrior should sing his death song when he knew his time had come. I had never learned one, but I managed to sing the "dream song" I had received in a dream vision when I lived among the Lenapes.

At this there was a murmur in the crowd around the scaffold. In a sort of daze I saw them, dim shapes, filing by to stare at me. Suddenly one stopped; I could see again; there stood a tall, slender girl, whose hair, shorter than most, hung only to her shoulders. She lingered, looking into my eyes, as if she was determined to see right through them into my soul itself and said something I could not understand.

Those coming behind murmured at the delay and she went on, with several backward looks which my eyes met. I felt, somehow, that she pitied me deeply; and in spite of agonizing wrists and aching limbs I watched until she disappeared into the crowd.

Shortly afterwards I was startled to see her back again, this time with a big, moon-faced woman. Both of them spoke directly to my captor, who was standing beside me on the platform. He grunted angrily and gave an order to his men; I saw them hand him bundles of splinters and a lighted torch! I remembered the Iroquois torture stories; how they punched holes in a captive's flesh and inserted burning splinters. How could I stand that? Could I die bravely and silently as a warrior should, or would I shriek and cry? Again I sang my "dream song." Somehow I gained courage. I would show them how a Lenape could die! I forgot entirely that I was English by birth.

A woman's harsh and scolding voice brought me back to earth; a square-chinned old woman with bright black eyes was now standing beside the short-haired girl and Moon-Face, lecturing the old devil who had captured me. He stood it for a while with averted face, as I watched with dawning hope; finally with a growl he flung the torch as far as he could, and stepped back out

of my sight. Then I heard him getting down from the
platform; his men exchanged a few words among themselves; then they, too, departed.

Now Short-Hair and Moon-Face came scrambling
up on the scaffold; the old woman helped them; they cut
the thongs that bound me to the frame; I collapsed in a
heap. Dimly I remember hands on my shoulders, words
in a strange tongue—and I knew no more.

The shock of cold water revived me; I found my-

self in the clutches of four strong, middle-aged women, standing breast deep in a small river or creek. When they saw me coming to, they laughed and cackled and plunged me beneath the water until I thought they were trying to drown me. Then they scrubbed me with sand and scouring rushes like a dirty kettle; it is a wonder I had any skin left when at last they dragged me to the bank.

Short-Hair was waiting, and she took me by the arm. I went with her willingly, for I knew she had saved my life. I thanked her in Lenape; smiling, she said something in her own tongue, but of course neither of us understood a word the other said. Her mouth was not as small as White-Deer's perhaps, but her teeth were white and even, and her lips well formed. Moreover she had pretty dimples when she smiled. At that time, in June 1616, I had passed my eighteenth birthday; her age appeared to be about the same.

She led me to one of the large houses covered with sheets of bark; it was almost as wide as the Lenape Big-House where they hold their worship, but much longer, perhaps fifty paces or more. We entered at one end, passing through a covered vestibule where stood several large wooden mortars for grinding corn. We then went into the building proper and stood in a room that was full of bark barrels. The walls and even the ceiling poles were hung with strings of corn on the ear and strips of dried pumpkin or squash.

From this point I could see a wide hallway stretching toward the other end of the building, with fires burning in it in several places. Down this corridor we walked, and now I found that the house was divided up into compartments on both sides of the hallway, with a family living in each. The women stared as we passed and some of the children followed us. The fourth compartment was vacant on both sides, and here we turned in to the right. There were three bunks built against the outside wall, each with a sort of upper story, and all bare of bedding. Short-Hair seated me on the first and signing me to wait, she disappeared leaving two naked little boys and four girls in short skirts, aged from three to nine, standing solemnly, and staring at me.

Soon she was back with her arms full of mats and skin robes; she made up the middle bed, and even fixed a curtain of soft-tanned skin which she showed me how to draw across the front. Now she led me over and sat me on the edge of the bunk she had made up, then brought me a big wooden bowl full of hulled corn, meat and beans all cooked together. I never tasted anything better.

The only light in the compartment came in through the smoke hole over the fireplace in the middle of the hallway. Now this light was fading and evening was at hand. Short-Hair brought coals from somewhere in a piece of broken clay kettle and started a fire in this section of the corridor. When its light filled the compartment, she came over and sat down by my side. For the first time she took note of the ogling children, and spoke sharply to them. One little boy wrinkled up his nose and made what sounded like a saucy reply, but the youngsters withdrew.

Now Short-Hair turned to me with a sort of admiring look that somehow embarrassed me. She picked up my hands and inspected the sore places on my wrists where the thongs had torn the skin, and caressed them gently. We heard someone coming along the corridor, and she let go of my hands just as one of the ugliest human beings I ever saw, entered the compartment; a humpbacked dwarf not much more than four feet tall, but with the arms and shoulders of a strong man. His eyes were tiny, his mouth huge, his nose enormous, shaped like a turnip.

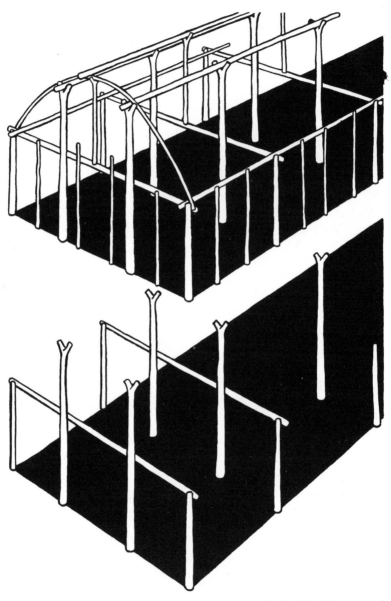

A simplified diagram of

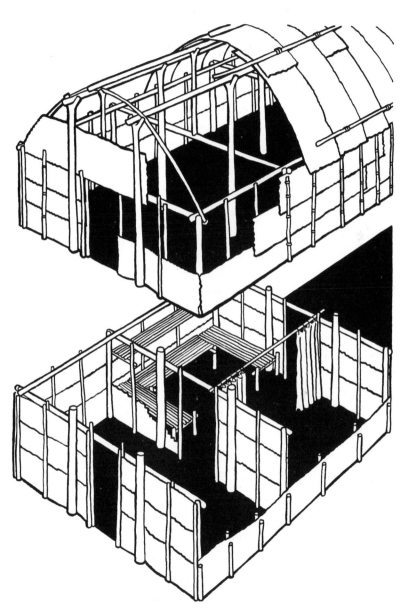

Iroquois long-house construction.

Behind him came the square-jawed old lady with the bright black eyes who had lectured my captor. Now I saw that the dwarf was carrying my bow and quiver of arrows, also a bundle. She spoke to him sternly and pointed to me. Glaring at me and growling like a bear the creature laid the things on my bunk and scuttled out.

Short-Hair opened the bundle. The cover of it was my robe; inside, besides my leggings and moccasins, lay my two shoulder pouches, my knife, my war club and best of all, my hunting charm and "dream bundle." While living among the Lenapes, I was required, as is customary for boys upon reaching a certain age, to go alone into the wilderness to fast and pray for power. They believe that any beings who may appear in dreams or visions at this time become his spirit helpers, something like guardian angels.

In my dream men and women came out of the forest bringing me food in bowls and giving me several articles —a flint-chipping tool of deer's horn, a sewing awl of bone and a wooden war club. It was only when they turned to go that I saw they were huge ants instead of people.

I had no idea what this dream might mean until Roaring-Wings explained it to me. He said the war club was a promise of power to fight, while the chipper and the awl meant that I was given skill to work; and the bowls of food, that through my work I would live in plenty. The old man made me a tiny club, chipper and awl which he put in a pouch for me to carry that I might not forget these promises; and this is what I call my "dream bundle." In a later dream, the ants taught me a song and this is the one I sang when tied to the torture frame, and which I call my "dream song."

Now all my possessions had come back to me except the dog Moonhakee. He had probably been killed when he tried to rescue me, I thought.

Short-Hair examined each article carefully, studying the workmanship, so different, in many cases, from that of her own people. Only the "dream bundle" was excepted; that she handed to me at once. It was plain that she felt there was something sacred and personal about it.

The two women talked together a while—I think they were discussing me, from the glances they shot in my direction. Then the old lady took her leave. I slipped on leggings and moccasins, hung my bow and quiver on a peg, and arranged my other things on the upper bunk above my bed. Now I realized that I was very, very tired, and that bed looked most inviting.

But this was not the end yet. Moon-Face appeared and beckoned Short-Hair and me to follow. The big woman led the way out of the house, through the village to the public square. Smoke was rising from the houses against the evening sky; doorways glowed with firelight from within; people were laughing and talking, children shouting, dogs barking. She led us across the square to a building near its center, almost as large as the long-houses where they lived, but without bunks or partitions. In fact the floor was entirely clear except for two fire pits, one near each end; and I realized this was a public meeting place even before I noticed the two rows of pole benches along the walls which must have furnished seats for many people.

Now I noticed in the flickering firelight that the seats at one end of the building were occupied, and more men and women were coming in. Moon-Face escorted us there and someone spread a mat for us to sit on the floor near the fire pit where all could see, while the people chatted and stared at us curiously. Suddenly the talk stopped as a tall, hawk-faced man strode into the building and up to where we sat. The two women rose hastily, and I followed their example.

Pointing to myself, to Short-Hair and to Moon-Face in turn the man addressed the people, making what sounded like a flowery speech, although I could not understand a word; then Moon-Face took the floor.

There was one word, *Hah-nya-denh-goh'-nah,* that she repeated several times, so distinctly that I remembered it; then she took me by the arm and led me completely around the floor, back to the starting point. This made me think of my adoption as a Lenape. Could this, too, be an adoption ceremony?

When Moon-Face finished, an old man rose to his feet. *"Waaah,"* he whooped, in a high, piercing tone, and the people responded, *"Wuh! Wuh! Waaah!"* as he stepped out from his place and took me by the arm.

Now he started to walk me up and down the council-house floor while he sang a funny little song and the people kept time to our steps with *"heh, heh, heh."* As he finished he shouted, *"Un-hay-yay-way wuh!"* and the crowd responded, *"Wuh! Wuh! Waaah!"*

Now another man took me in charge, singing a different song, to which the people responded as before; then another and another. Finally, when no more singers stepped forward, the hawk-faced man, whom I took to be a chief, laid his hand on my shoulder and addressed me, using the word, *Hah-nya-denh-goh'-nah,* which, I felt, must be my new name.

After we left the building, Short-Hair simply whispered the word *"Oh-neh'"* and disappeared into the darkness. I thought the word must mean "good night," but found out later that it simply means "now," short for "now I am going," and the answer is *"nyoh!"* meaning "so be it!"

I followed Moon-Face with some misgivings, thinking of my belongings left behind in Short-Hair's house, not to speak of the tempting bed; but she led me to her own compartment in another long-house, introduced me to a sour-faced man I took to be her husband, and to a stout old lady who sat near, as *Hah-nya-denh-goh'-nah.* The man, after glancing at me skeptically, turned back to filling his pipe; but the plump one struggled to her feet and waddling over to where I stood, looked me over at short range.

Evidently she could not see very well in the dim firelight, but she exclaimed and chattered enthusiastically, which drew from the man a disgusted grunt. Then Moon-Face led me to a fairly comfortable bunk where I soon forgot my adventures.

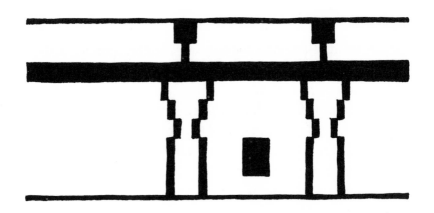

IV. MANY-TONGUES AND THE IROQUOIS TRAIL

Before daylight I awakened and could not sleep again. Someone in the compartment was snoring loudly, but that was not the reason. I was thinking of what had happened, wondering why I had been rescued; what might be in store for me. I twisted and squirmed. Finally the sky, seen through the smoke hole, began to brighten with the dawn, and shortly I could dimly see the inside of the compartment.

I rose to go out, thinking to return to the other long-house where my things had been left; but as I passed Moon-Face's bed a hand reached out and stopped me.

Then Moon-Face sat up and spoke to me earnestly, but of course I could not understand. Seeing this she made signs until I finally gathered that I should return shortly for breakfast. Out I went, noticing as I passed that families in other compartments were stirring. In the vestibule at the end of the building two women had already begun to pound corn in big wooden mortars, making a hollow thumping.

I stepped forth. The whole eastern sky was ablaze with pink and red clouds. Standing there enchanted, I was suddenly jarred by the uproar of a terrific dogfight. Hurrying around the corner of the house, I found Moonhakee battling the biggest dog of a pack that had evidently attacked him. Before I could interfere the strange dog fled yelping, and his friends followed.

Moonhakee, limping a little, approached me very humbly as if begging my forgiveness for being away so long. I petted him, thankful to see him alive after all; then went down to the creek and washed, while early risers watched me curiously. Finally I returned to the house, Moonhakee at my heels. As I entered the compartment Moon-Face's husband, seeing a strange dog following me, picked up a stick of firewood. I hastened to point to Moonhakee, then to myself. He threw down the stick with a wry grin.

Hardly had I sat down on the edge of my bed, with Moonhakee at my feet, when in walked Short-Hair, followed by a sturdy boy perhaps fourteen years old. They were carrying my things which had been left in the other long-house.

They came over and laid my treasures on the bed beside me, and she said something to me, which of course I did not understand, but I thanked her in Lenape. By the time they had found seats, Moon-Face was ready to serve breakfast. She gave us each a wooden bowl filled with steaming hominy cooked with meat, a carved wooden spoon and a round cake of heavy boiled bread with berries mixed in. Even Moonhakee was served a bone with quite a lot of meat.

I knew they were discussing me during the meal; they could hardly take their eyes off me, or stop talking long enough to eat. As for myself, I filled my stomach while I had the chance, not knowing when I might get another meal like this.

Finally the boy laid down his bowl and wiping his mouth with the back of his hand, came over and sat down beside me. Studying me with snappy black eyes for a moment, he asked, in perfectly good Lenape, "What village was your home?"

I nearly fell off the bed! Finally I managed to respond "Turtle-Town. What village did you come from?"

Passing over my question he asked me another.

"Why did you come here?"

I explained as carefully and truthfully as I could, and the boy spoke to the others, probably interpreting what I said, because they looked relieved. Now it was my turn to ask questions.

"How did you guess that I speak Lenape?"

"You are dressed like a Lenape," he replied, "but we thought at first that you might be one of our own people come back from another world. You look very much like one of our young men who was killed in war about a year ago. He was the son of this woman here," pointing to Moon-Face, "and this girl here was going to marry him." He pointed to Short-Hair.

"Is-is that why they rescued me?" I stammered.

The boy talked to the women a few minutes, then turned back to me.

"The girl says when she saw you hanging on that torture frame, something seemed to tell her that she should save you. Our women have the right to adopt captives to take the place of dead relatives. She had lost the man she had expected to marry, but he was no blood kin of course. So she had to go to his mother," he pointed again to Moon-Face, "and it was she who claimed you to take his place as her son."

Moon-Face then spoke up, and the boy translated.

"You look so much like my son who was killed that I thought you might be he, come back from another world. I know your eyes are a lighter color, and your skin paler and hair faded looking, but I thought maybe that is what happens to people who die and come back again to life. What made us doubtful was this—you dress like a Lenape and do not speak our language. Anyhow, you looked too much like my son to allow you to be killed when we could save you."

That was an amazing story. I had known, of course, that somehow I owed my life to those two women, but I did not know how or why.

"It was a wonderful thing for them to do," I said, "and I am deeply grateful to them both." Then, remembering that among the Lenapes captives not put to death are held as slaves or servants, at least for a while, I asked, "Whose servant, then, am I?"

The boy did not even have to inquire.

"You are not a servant. You were adopted yesterday in that ceremony. You are now this woman's son, and that man is your father. Some day," he added with a grin, "after you get to know her better, and if you prove worthy, you may be lucky enough to marry this girl. She cut her hair in mourning for the lad who was killed but I think she will let it grow now."

I looked at Short-Hair, but she turned her face quickly away. Perhaps she knew in advance what the boy was going to tell me.

What should I do? I owed my life to these women, my very life—I must not do anything to hurt them. Yet I could not forget poor Little-Bear, held as a hostage among the Iroquois, while his family suffered, back there in Lenape land. So I told them what was on my mind.

"If I am not a servant, I should like to carry out the errand that brought me here. Yet I owe everything to these two good women; truly my life belongs to them; and I'd like to know what they think about it."

The boy interpreted, and that started a flood of talk. Moon-Face's husband—my new father—said nothing, except one growling remark with a disgusted air; the boy, at one point said something and pointed to himself. I was wondering if the talk would ever cease, when he turned again to me.

"It's all fixed," he said. "They are sorry you feel you must do this thing, but they understand how you feel. One great trouble is, you cannot speak the language of any of the tribes you will meet. On that account, I am going along to talk for you. Then they think some older person ought to go with you also—it would be safer. Your new mother says she will go. Her husband objected, but the girl says she will come and cook for him and your grandmother while we are gone, so he is satisfied."

Then Short-Hair spoke, looking at the ground the while.

"She says she would like to go with you, but it would not be right unless you and she were married."

I could think of nothing to say to that, so I changed the subject.

"What is her name?" I asked.

"*Ah-wen-hah-gon'-wah* in our language," he replied. "That means 'Among-the-Blossoms.'"

Again the girl spoke.

"She wants to know what your name was before we adopted you."

I never thought of my English name—Richard Sherwood or "Dickon" so I told them my Lenape name— *Day'-kay-ning* or "In-the-Forest."

Then I learned that my new father was *Day-hat-kah'-dons* or "Looks-Both-Ways," a chief of the Beaver Clan; and that my new mother, whom I had thought of as "Moon-Face" was really *Goon-wah-hah'-wee,* meaning "She-Carries-It-Along" or "Carrying-Woman."

Now the old lady spoke up—they all looked at her in surprise. The boy whispered, "She says it's not right to make the girl stay here when she has just saved your life. You two should have the chance to get acquainted, she says.

"The grandma is not too old to cook, she claims; maybe she can still beat the girl at cooking. Anyhow she will take care of Looks-Both-Ways, so the girl can

go with you. People will not make bad talk with Carrying-Woman along."

She and Short-Hair—I mean Among-the-Blossoms
—went over to Grandma, caressed her hands, thanked
her; and even Looks-Both-Ways spoke kindly to her.
Then Carrying-Woman addressed me.

"She is asking when you wish to start on your trip."

Rather taken aback, I answered, "Any time! The
sooner the better!"

Life is strange. Yesterday I was about to die by torture at the hands of the Iroquois; today an Iroquois was
inquiring my wishes! I was not sure I liked the idea of
taking the girl along, but what could I say? After speaking to the boy the two women left the compartment.

"They are going to tell the girl's mother about the
trip," the boy explained. "They will pick up the things
she will need on the journey."

Grandma pulled a pack basket from under a bunk
and departed. Looks-Both-Ways gloomily took down his
bow and quiver from a peg, then addressed me while
the boy interpreted.

"My wife has adopted you, and even her mother
has accepted so I suppose I shall have to call you 'son,' "
he grumbled. "Maybe if you ever learn my language
I'll like you better. It is late, the sun is already high, but
perhaps I can still find a deer. We have a new mouth to
feed." Tall, thin, sour-faced, he left the compartment.
The boy and I were alone.

"Bet he doesn't find a deer," the boy chuckled. "Your
new father is a wise chief, but as a deer hunter he's not
too good."

"Please explain what happened after I was rescued," I begged.

"Carrying-Woman hurried around and called a meeting of the Turtle Clan, to which she belongs, to adopt you before anything else happened. Some were against it, but she persuaded them. Oh, that woman can do anything! A clan chief directed the ceremony and several members led you around, singing their 'joy-songs' to give you good luck. They named you 'Big-Turtle' which is an old name belonging to the clan. It seemed to fit you because of the turtle tattooed on your chest."

This turtle, together with two figures of ants he did not mention, were relics of my stay among the Lenapes. They seemed now almost childish compared to the fancy tattooed designs I saw covering the necks, arms and chests of so many Iroquois men. However, I can say one thing for the simple Lenape tattoo patterns—you can tell at a glance what they represent. But not so the Iroquois.

So I now belonged to the Turtle Clan. I sat for a few moments thinking things over. Finally I said to the boy:

"Now I'd like to ask about you. What's your name, and how did a Lenape boy your age ever get up into this Iroquois country?"

He laughed. "Truly, I am not a Lenape," he said. "I was born right here in this town of *Gah-nah-dah-go'-nah*. My real name is *Day-weh-nee-do'-geh*—'Between-Two-Moons'—but everybody calls me *Hoh-nah-sah-gah'-deh* or 'Many-Tongues' because I can learn different languages easily. I learned Lenape from a captive woman right here in this town. I can speak the languages of all

our Five Nations which are somewhat alike, and besides
Lenape itself the languages of several other Bark-Eater *
tribes to the east of us, all cousins of the Lenapes, I think.
Anyhow their talk is very different from ours.

"My father and mother are dead. Part of the time
I live with one aunt, part with the other. Some day I
shall have a big name. Already the chiefs call me into
council to interpret for them. Anything more you wish to
know about me?" He chuckled saucily.

"That's enough for now. What about this girl who
saved me?"

"Among-the-Blossoms was born here, one of our own
On-on-da-geh-hay'-nah or Hill People—one of our Five
Nations of Long-House Builders. She is living with her
mother who is a widow. They have plenty of corn, which
they raise themselves, of course, but there is no one to
hunt meat for them. When they get too meat-hungry,
Among-the-Blossoms goes out hunting herself."

"I never heard of such a thing." I cried, half shocked.
"I never knew a girl or woman who even knew how to
hold a bow!"

"This girl knows—never fear," said the boy. "But
I don't think she likes to hunt. Maybe now you can hunt
deer for them. What's the matter with your ears? They
look red!"

I felt we were getting into deep water, so I changed
the subject.

"Who is that terrible old man who captured me?"

* For some reason the Iroquois call the Lenape group of tribes by
a name which means "They-Eat-Bark." The Mohawk form of this which
might be written *Hah-tee-roon'-taks* is the origin of the name "Adiron-
dacks" for a range of mountains.

"You should feel honored," he replied, "to be captured by the famous Onondaga chief Tadoda'ho (*Tahdo-dah'-ho*) known as 'Snakes-Around-His-Head,' now Grand Chief of all the united Five Nations. He is indeed terrible, and all people fear him, even though, as Grand Chief, he isn't allowed to go to war any more."

"There was one person who did not fear him," I objected. "The old woman who was scolding him that day."

"That was his wife," he laughed. "I forgot her. You are right, she's not afraid of him. She told him that even he might lose his horns if he kept on breaking the rules."

"Lose his horns?"

"Yes, that means lose his office as Chief. As I told you, our women have the right to claim captives to take the place of dead relatives. Carrying-Woman claimed you to take the place of her dead son, but Tadoda'ho was so set on torturing you that he paid no attention. He argued that you were a spy for a tribe of light-skinned wizards * who have been helping our northern enemies of late. But his wife made him follow the rules."

"Who was that ugly dwarf who brought me my things last night?"

"Oh, that's *Ho-nyuh-sah-go'-nah*, which means 'Big-Nose'; he's Tadoda'ho's servant and messenger. When he's home, he takes care of the snakes."

"What snakes?"

"The snakes Tadoda'ho wears tied in his hair to frighten people. You didn't think they grew out of the old man's head, did you? Big-Nose keeps them in a spe-

* He was referring to the French who had been allied with the Hurons.

cial basket and they say he feeds them mice and frogs."

I did not wish to admit that the snakes had fooled me, so I changed the subject again.

"Big-Nose looks dangerous, but not very smart," I said.

"He is smarter than people think, and just as mean as his master; but the old lady tells him what to do, too. She saw to it that you received your belongings."

Just then my new mother and the girl came in carrying a lot of stuff which they piled in a corner; then Carrying-Woman spoke to the boy, pointing to the bunk in the corner of the apartment.

"She says she wants to fix you up properly. You belong to our tribe now and should wear our clothes." He climbed up on the bunk and peered into its upper shelf, finally reaching over and dragging out a large boxlike basket with a cover, the kind these people (and the Lenapes, too) keep their best clothes in. He carried it over and set it down before me. I happened to glance at the women. My new mother was wiping her eyes and the girl looked very solemn.

"These are the dead son's clothes," Many-Tongues explained as he opened the basket. "Now since you are taking up his name again and his place in the tribe, Carrying-Woman thought you should have them. She says, put on a pair of the leggings."

I looked into the basket with the strangest feeling. A dead man's clothes! Well, but for these two dear women I would be dead myself now. Many-Tongues helped me spread the garments out, shaking off the dust. The women left hurriedly; I imagine the sight of the well-remembered clothing was too much for them.

There were three pairs of leggings, one of them very fancy, with fine embroidery—all sorts of pretty little curlicues, embroidered in dyed deer hair, red, yellow and black. None of the leggings had side fringes like the Lenape style, and the seams all ran up the front. From the tops where the belt straps were attached, embroidered deerskin strips dangled down to the knee. I picked out the plainest pair and changed. They fitted me pretty well. The dead son, I reflected, must have been just about my size.

There was also a new pair of moccasins puckered to one seam in front very much like Lenape style; but the flaps were covered with the same curlicue designs instead of straight lines and angles such as you would see in Lenape embroidery. These moccasins I put on; my old ones were nearly worn out, anyway.

We also found several short skirts or kilts, a plain deerskin robe, a beautiful embroidered robe and two fur sleeves. Moths or bugs had started to eat the fur on the last, so Many-Tongues turned them inside out and brushed them.

"I'll take these out and hang them in the sun a while," he said. "You will be glad to have them next winter."

In a few minutes he was back, bringing the women with him. They seemed to feel better, but I noticed they kept their eyes turned away from the clothes, as we gathered them up and put them back in their basket.

Once the lid was on, Carrying-Woman spoke.

"The next thing, she says, is to fix your hair in Iroquois style. You are not going to enjoy this," he added with a chuckle.

She unrolled a rush mat on the floor and seated herself on one end, beckoning me to come; in a moment I was stretched out on the mat with my head in her lap, while Among-the-Blossoms brought a wooden bowl of water and a bark tray of ashes from the fire pit, setting them down near my head.

I knew it was going to be a painful ordeal—and it was. First Carrying-Woman dampened her fingers, then dipped them in ashes to give a better grip, then seized a little pinch of my hair and gave a quick jerk! Did it hurt! Then she pulled out another wisp and another. By the time she had finished all my hair, which was quite long, had been pulled out except a round patch at the crown, which was left for a scalp lock, to be worn loose. My whole head was as sore as a boil, but she rubbed it with bear's grease and after a few days the soreness was gone.

"Now you are truly *On'-gweh On'-weh*," joked Many-Tongues. "Especially since those four women scrubbed the Bark-Eater smell off you when they had you in the creek." *On'-gweh On'-weh* means "person-real" and these Long-House Builders use it as a name for their own people. They pretend not to recognize members of other tribes as "real persons."

While she was fixing my hair my new mother noticed that my ears were pierced, so she got out a pair of shell ear pendants and hung them to my ears with deerskin thongs.

Next she sent me out hunting, with Many-Tongues as guide, and we succeeded in killing two deer. When these were brought in, Looks-Both-Ways hardly knew what to think, as his own hunt had been a failure. He called me to him, and the boy came along to interpret.

"Tell me, Son," he said, "do you by any chance possess a hunting charm?"

I showed him the little wooden face I usually carry strung around my neck while I am hunting—made for me by the Lenape doctor, Roaring-Wings. It represents the spirit *Mee-sing-haw-lee'-kun,* who is said to be guardian of game animals.

"This looks like a pretty girl compared to our wooden faces," he really grinned. "Will you lend it to me for tomorrow's hunt?"

I let him have it, and my new father, starting out at dawn, actually killed two deer himself that day—something he had not done for years. He might look sour, he might grumble, but he was my friend from that time on, even though I could not, at the start, speak his language.

We traded three of the deer, skins and all, for dried meat, leaving the fourth for Looks-Both-Ways and Grandma.

While the hunting was in progress, Carrying-Woman and Among-the-Blossoms made us all some extra moccasins, then prepared as much parched corn as they thought we could carry.

I watched them while they dragged hot coals out of the fire with sticks, and set over them large pieces of broken earthen pots. Into these shallow bowls they poured the shelled corn, and stirred it around until it was toasted. Then they poured it into a big wooden bowl and repeated. When the bowl was full, I followed them out to the vestibule and watched the next step: they pounded the toasted corn in big wooden mortars with long wooden pestles until it would run through a fine basket sieve. The last thing they did was to mix in a little tree (maple) sugar and pour the mixture into a deer-skin sack which was tied up tight to keep out the ants.

To get a tasty and satisfying meal in a hurry, all that is necessary is to mix this stuff with water. In Onondaga it is called *o-nen'-ha o-non'-deh* or *o-nen-hon'-deh;* in Lenape *ka-ha-ma'-kun.* Hunters, warriors, travelers, all carry it.

Everything went smoothly until the evening before we had planned to start. The six of us were sitting very happily in our compartment, talking over plans for the morrow, when Tadoda'ho's wife slipped in and called the women off to one side. They whispered a moment and then the old lady departed as silently as she had come.

She had brought us bad news. Tadoda'ho was bitter against us for having shamed him before the people, and he had vowed to get even, which might mean anything up to murder. The old lady warned us to be always on guard. I could not sleep that night, and I doubt if my companions did any better.

I was just dozing off toward morning when Carrying-Woman shook me. She had everything ready—all our food, our clay cooking kettles, wooden food bowls and spoons, spare moccasins and even robes, all packed on two burden frames which she proposed for herself and Among-the-Blossoms to carry, leaving to Many-Tongues and me only our weapons.

I was trying to make her understand by signs that I wished to carry my share of the load, when Many-Tongues, who had slipped out to take leave of his aunts, came in. At once my new mother poured out a torrent of words, and Among-the-Blossoms joined.

"Your mother says," he translated, "that we men-folk must not carry anything. It is our task to furnish the party with fresh meat and to defend us, and that is enough."

That was an argument hard to answer; but I had my way to this extent—Many-Tongues carried the robes, done up in a bundle on his back. I thought best to divide the weapons so that each would have some means of defense: I, of course, took the bow and arrows; Many-Tongues my war club and Among-the-Blossoms my long flint knife. I had given my English knife to my Lenape foster-mother at Turtle-Town.

Carrying-Woman produced her own axe, of which I could see she was very proud. "This is the only weapon I'll ever need," she said, fondling the green stone blade. "I'm sorry for anyone who tries to attack us!"

It really was a fine one, I'll admit, with a sharp wedge-shaped blade set in a clublike handle of polished hardwood. It was almost exactly like a Lenape man's axe. After some talk I learned that this was the only kind of axe the Iroquois used, disdaining the Lenape woman's axe with its grooved stone blade.

When the women had rearranged their loads and tied them fast, my new mother led me close to the fire, then stood back to look me over. Now she spoke and Many-Tongues interpreted.

"Your mother says she gave you some good clothes;

why don't you wear them? She wants you to look nice so she can be proud of you."

To tell the truth I had been so worried I had not thought much about my clothes; but I said (which was true), "I heard rain on the roof last night. Mud would spoil all that pretty fancy-work in no time."

The two talked together and then the boy said:

"She wishes you to wear one of the kilts anyhow so you will look more *On'-gweh On'-weh.*"

"I thought those little skirts were for girls!" I protested.

"No, our men wear them often. Haven't you seen them?"

So the square basket had to be taken down again, and Many-Tongues dragged out one of the plainest kilts. For Carrying-Woman's sake I put it on, although it was a real skirt of deerskin, fringed around the bottom and reaching nearly to my knees. I consoled myself by thinking of the kilts worn by the bold Scottish Highlanders. Iroquois women's skirts are different anyhow; for one thing they are much longer, reaching nearly to the ankles.

We left the village just as dawn was breaking over the wooded hilltop to the east, where I had been captured. There was no sunrise however, for the sky was dark and threatening, matching my gloomy thoughts of the trouble with Tadoda'ho, that seemed bound to come, sooner or later.

Our route led north down the valley, with the river on our left for some distance; then we swung away from the stream and soon came upon a much traveled path running east and west, with marked trees on both sides, and so old the foot-wide trail was worn ankle-deep into the ground in some places. Through brush it ran like a tunnel, high enough to clear a man's feathers, wide enough for elbows and pack frames.

A statement that the Lenape hostages had been taken "toward the setting sun"—the only information Carrying-Woman had been able to extract from her tribesmen—was all we had to guide us, so we turned west on the old trail with some hesitation.

I would have enjoyed seeing the oldest Onondaga town, which stood on a hilltop a few leagues to the northeast; but it is lucky we turned west, as we discovered later. Soon we came to the river again, at a shallow ford where the trail crossed.

Once over the river we passed through a small and rather scattered Onondaga village, and soon after made our way up through a ravine out of the valley. The water from last night's rain still stood in puddles in the trail. Carefree Moonhakee seemed to enjoy splashing through them; but as we slopped along with wet feet I was still thinking about Tadoda'ho and his threat to our plans.

Finally I said to Many-Tongues:

"If old Tadoda'ho is so mean, and powerful, and is so bitter against us, why doesn't he have us killed outright and get rid of us?"

The boy talked with Carrying-Woman a few minutes; then he said:

"The old man is afraid of losing his horns. If he could put us out of the way without anyone knowing he was back of it, no doubt he would try. But if his Head Matron heard of it, his horns would be gone."

"Do you mean to tell me that a woman can pull down the Grand Chief of the Five Nations?" It seemed to me very strange; I knew women in England have no such power.

"Truly!" he replied. "The women of an *oh-wah'-jee-yah,* of whom the Head Matron is leader, not only have power to throw out an old chief, but to name a new one in his place!"

"What is an *oh-wah'-jee-yah?*"

"It's like a big family of people related to each other through their mothers. Each clan is made up of one or more of them. I don't know how many times the Head Matron of Tadoda'ho's *oh-wah'-jee-yah,* which belongs to the Bear Clan, has warned him to 'Step back into the path.' The only reason she has been so patient is that he has been so useful to the League."

"Useful? How could such a wicked man be useful?"

"Since he has been Grand Chief, peace has come to the land. No enemy dares attack us now, or very seldom. Before the Five Nations joined hands my uncle says a year never passed without raids from enemy tribes. Now, even a small party like ours can travel this trail from one end to the other without danger."

"Why, then," I demanded, "is my new mother carrying her axe in her hand and not in her pack?"

The boy grinned ruefully.

"Maybe I should have said 'without danger from outside enemies.' But don't think Tadoda'ho started the League. My uncle says he was against it at first. They say it was Deganawida's * idea and that Hiawatha * worked on it with him. But Tadoda'ho planted thorn bushes in their path and they could make no headway. Finally Jigon'sasay (*Jee-gon'-sah-say*) the Mother of Nations, helped them; she showed them how to comb the snakes out of Tadoda'ho's hair. Then Tadoda'ho uprooted the thorn bushes and the road was open for the Five Nations to get together and build one big Long-House in which they all could live and raise their children in peace. Anyhow, that's what my uncle says."

"That does not make sense," I complained. "What do you mean?"

Many-Tongues laughed. "That's our way of talking. You will have to sharpen your wits if you wish to be an Iroquois."

That nettled me and I walked along a while in silence, thinking over what he had said. Then it began to

* Pronounced *Day-gah-nah-wee'-dah* and *Hah-yah-went'-hah*.

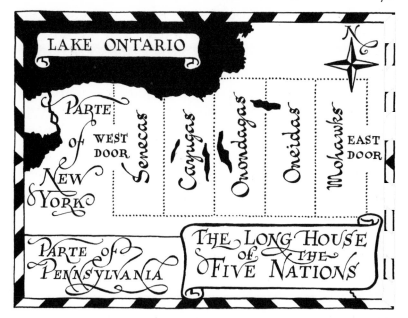

dawn on me what he meant. "Why did Tadoda'ho plant the thorn bushes?" I asked.

"Well, he was already a leading chief of the Onondagas, and he feared that if the League were formed he would be only one little chief among five."

"How did what's-her-name, the Mother of Nations, suggest that they comb the snakes out of his hair?"

"She advised that Tadoda'ho be offered the position of Grand Chief or Fire-Keeper of all the united Five Nations; that would give him more power instead of less. Or so my uncle tells."

"They did build a big Long-House, didn't they?" I went on to show I really understood.

"Truly! Uncle says it takes many days to walk from one end to the other. The eastern door is on the River

of the Mahikans (Hudson) and its keepers are the Flint
People (Mohawks); the western door is at the valley of
Jon-nes'-see-yoh (Genessee) and its keepers are the Big
Mountain People (Senecas). We, the Hill People (On-
ondagas), live in the middle and keep the Council Fire."

"That's three of the Five Nations," I said. "Who
are the other two?"

"The Standing Stone People (Oneidas) east of us,
and the Canoe Portage People (Cayugas) to the west.
We should arrive in one of their villages some time tomorrow. And now I am going to tell you something else,"
the boy went on, "since you are smart enough to understand what I said about the Long-House. Often my uncle
repeats it in this way:

" 'The Five Nations dug a great hole, and in it they
buried all their weapons of war. Above these they planted
a Tree of Peace with long leaves. In its top they set an
eagle to watch in all directions and give warning of the
approach of any enemy who might try to cut down the
Tree.

" 'The Tree of Peace grew and grew, and all the
Five Nations seated themselves beneath its pleasant shade.
When they saw that there was plenty of room, they invited other nations to join them under the spreading
branches.' "

"I think I understand," I said. "The idea is a noble
one, and I should like to learn more about it. They know
something of it in Turtle-Town."

"You will learn," said Many-Tongues.

After a while the sun came out very hot; the wet
earth fairly steamed. Still going northwest, we came, late

in the morning, to a creek and after crossing this swung west again.

Many-Tongues and I chattered in Lenape about this and that until I happened to catch a glimpse of the women's sweat-streaked faces as they trudged along with their heavy burdens. They looked sour enough—and with good reason. Naturally they felt left out when we jabbered away in a strange tongue and did not interpret.

I passed the word to the boy, who explained to them that he had been telling me about the League; but they made no response, and the four of us trudged along in silence. Little we knew what strange adventure was soon to befall us.

V. I PLAY DOCTOR

The day continued hot, without even a breeze; but black thunderclouds were piling up in the west. We dragged through the hot and breathless forest, over hill and dale, until we were ready to drop. Late in the afternoon we heard the sound of rushing water and came suddenly upon a creek foaming down over the rocks and disappearing into the brush on the right. The ground was smooth under a large tree and here we settled down to rest and cool off, the women taking off their burden frames, the boy his bundle.

Carrying-Woman stretched out for a nap, her axe close at hand, I noticed; but Among-the-Blossoms said she needed a bath and disappeared downstream, leaving Many-Tongues and me to talk Lenape to our hearts' content. Moonhakee lay down in the shallow water, panting.

It was then I took the opportunity to ask a delicate question.

"What about Among-the-Blossoms' mother? I have seen nothing of her at all; yet the two were living together before I was captured."

"Maybe she did not approve of her daughter's rescuing you," he replied, "and is keeping out of your sight for that reason. Or she may be one of those who think it is bad luck for a mother-in-law to have anything to do with her future son-in-law." He chuckled provokingly.

I decided not to pursue that subject further. So I proposed that he start teaching me the Onondaga language, and we were in the midst of the first lesson when we heard Among-the-Blossoms calling.

"What does she say?" I asked him.

"I can't exactly make out, but she is very angry about something."

"Why don't you go down and see what it is?" I demanded.

"Go yourself!" the boy grunted. "Don't you wear a warrior's scalp lock?" He looked really scared, himself, but he added, "What are you afraid of?"

I pushed through the bushes following the creek and came to quite a pool at the foot of a steep bluff, and here was a little beach. Among-the-Blossoms was standing breast-deep in the water, yelling and pointing. For a moment I did not grasp what was wrong; then I realized I could not see her clothes anywhere. I hurried back and got my robe out of Many-Tongues' pack. Carrying-Woman was awakened by the commotion, and the first thing she grabbed for was that axe! I gave her the robe to take down to Among-the-Blossoms, and we waited.

When the girl arrived, wrapped in my robe and followed by my new mother, they both began to scold.

"They say," he interpreted, "that we played a very mean joke on her by hiding her clothes when she was so tired. She wants us to give them to her at once!"

"Why, I don't know anything about it," I gasped.

"Neither do I, and that's what I am trying to tell them. We were just sitting here talking when we heard the girl call."

Among-the-Blossoms must have seen by my expression that we were telling the truth, and a frightened look came over her face. Who had taken her clothes? We all rushed down to the pool and looked about carefully. In a muddy spot near the water's edge was a single queer track, like the print of a crippled child's foot.

While we were puzzling over this, a crazy laugh cackled from the bluff above us, and a large stone flew through the air and landed at our feet. Moonhakee, shivering in spite of the heat, kept as close to us as he could.

Now we heard voices in the direction where we had left our baggage and ran back there, Carrying-Woman swinging her axe. Nothing had been harmed, but we heard a heavy something crashing off through the brush in the opposite direction. Whatever it was, Moonhakee would not pursue it—he, the dog that had grappled with bears and panthers back in Lenape land. Moreover, the rest of us felt the same way about it.

Among-the-Blossoms told us that while she was bathing she heard a rustling in the bushes on the other side of the pool, and some animal growling; she waded over to see what it was and when she turned back to the beach her clothes were gone.

"It must have been the Stone-Rollers," said Many-Tongues. "They are little people who live in the cliffs and rocks, and they love to play just such tricks."

"Are they real people like you and me?" I asked.

"Not exactly; they are more like spirits; they can show themselves or vanish whenever they please."

Whether such elves or goblins were to blame or not, Among-the-Blossoms' clothes were gone. Wishing to travel as light as possible we had brought no extra clothing except moccasins. While we were discussing what to do, the clouds were getting blacker overhead. Suddenly a crash of thunder echoed among the hills; big drops of rain began to patter down.

Many-Tongues thought he remembered passing the night in a bark shed a short distance up the creek, the last trip he made west; so we snatched up our things and hurried along, reaching the shed just as the downpour started. I could see it was a regular camping place for travelers along the trail, but the roof leaked badly.

Carrying-Woman picked a dry spot for our precious store of parched corn and dried venison; then we sat down to wait. We could hardly hear each other speak for the roar of the rain on the bark roof and the forest leaves. Before sunset the storm passed and the sky cleared; but it was hopeless to try to start a fire and we were thankful to eat cold parched corn mixed with water. I imagine we had walked twenty English miles or more that day.

In the morning we succeeded in kindling a fire with

our firesticks and enjoyed a hot breakfast; then we dried out our things. Among-the-Blossoms was going to cut up her own robe to make skirt, waist and leggings; but I insisted that she use mine because it was plain and made of four large deerskins, which would give her more material to work with. Anyhow (I told her) the weather was warm and I did not need it, even to wrap up in at night.

As she was wearing that very robe as her only covering at the time, Many-Tongues and I discreetly withdrew while she and Carrying-Woman were working. The boy borrowed my bow and arrows and went hunting, and I, armed with the war club, sunned myself within easy calling distance. After our adventure with the Stone-Roller goblins or whatever they were, I dared not leave "our women" unprotected, axe or no axe.

The sun was halfway up in the heavens when they called me to see the result of their labors. The sewing on the new leggings was not as fine as on the old, and there was no quill work or deer-hair embroidery of course, but the waist or cape and the wrap-around skirt were neatly cut and fringed. I thought they had done a wonderful job considering the short time spent, and the fact that all they had to work with were a few sharp flint flakes to cut the skin, a bone awl and a hank of deer sinew to make thread for sewing.

Many-Tongues came in with two rabbits just then, and the women insisted on cleaning them and broiling them at once so they would not spoil. We crossed a creek on a set of stepping stones, which is not often seen. And toward the middle of the afternoon we forded a river, the name of which I forget.

The sun was sinking low when we arrived on the shore of a beautiful lake which stretched away to the south as far as the eye could see; we were near the north end of it. Turning north along the shore we soon found ourselves approaching a village of the Canoe Portage People. Many-Tongues said it was called *Deh-yo-hay'-yo-go,* meaning "Floating Rushes." He added that there were several other villages around the lake; but the largest, a fortified town and the capital of what the English now call the Cayuga nation, lay on a creek some distance inland, perhaps half a day's journey from where we stood.

As we neared the houses we were startled to see two painted young warriors, fully armed, sitting under a tree watching the trail. They jumped up and confronted us, addressing themselves to me; but though I could not understand them, their words sounded more friendly than hostile.

"They say we are expected," Many-Tongues explained with a puzzled air, "and that we must follow them to the council house."

As we walked through the village I noticed that the houses on the side toward the lake were quite small and poor looking; those farther inland larger and better built, although I saw no long-houses. The council house was built of poles and covered with bark, similar in most respects to the Onondaga building where I was adopted, only smaller.

As we entered a woman relieved both our bearers of their pack frames and a warrior took our weapons; we followed our guides to one end of the building. Here, on a bench, sat a sad-faced middle-aged man, slowly fanning himself with a turkey-tail fan. I noticed his tattooing, while simple, was very well done; and his kilt, his leggings and his moccasins were plain but beautifully made.

At either side, at some distance, stood a bodyguard

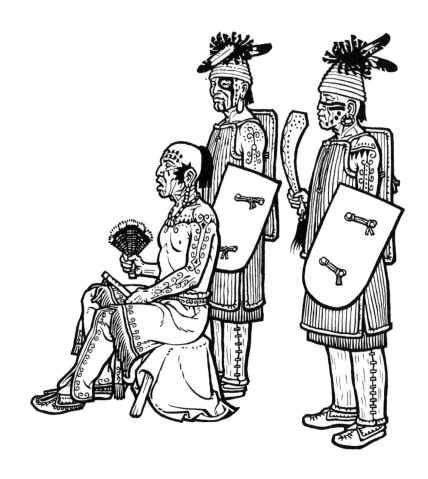

in strange dress, the two just alike; I had never seen this
before among the Indians. They were clad in armor; and
a rare armor it was, for the helmets were made of a thick
rope of grass or fiber, coiled about in the form of a cap,
and the coils sewed one tight to the other. These caps or
helmets looked thick enough and strong enough to break
the blow of a club or a stone hatchet, and were decked
with a bunch of split feathers at the top. For body armor
the guards wore sleeveless jackets or corselets of stout

wooden rods or slats fastened together with strong cords; and their shins were protected with armor made of thick bark; the upper part of their legs with aprons made of hardwood slats woven together with cords, front and back. Moreover they carried shields of oblong form, which appeared to be made of elm bark such as is used for house roofs and canoes, but thicker. They were armed with long flat clubs with one sharp edge, curved like a Turkish sword or scimitar.

This man wanted to make himself appear important by such a show of guards in livery or uniform, a thing rarely done by Indians, even the greatest chiefs. As for such armor, it might stop stone-pointed arrows, but never bullets.

The man looked up as we halted before him and spoke calmly and at some length.

When he finished, Many-Tongues, who had listened intently, turned to me with a puzzled face. "This chief says that a runner came in last night to announce our arrival, and told him all about us. You are a great Bark-Eater doctor, who has the power to cure any injury or disease. You even have the power to keep yourself and your family looking young, although you and your wife are quite old and your mother really aged. You may be recognized by the queer color of your eyes and your pale skin. It is your pleasure to speak only Lenape; your wife and your mother only Onondaga; but in truth the three of you can speak any language. The chief is very glad you came, for a certain reason."

I was so overwhelmed by this collection of lies that I did not try to deny them at the moment. Instead I asked, "Why is he glad we came?"

Another interchange of words.

"This is bad," warned Many-Tongues. "The chief says his only son fell out of a tree last spring and the boy's right arm has been helpless ever since. It pains and aches all the time, and now it has begun to wither. Three doctors have tried to cure the child, and all have failed. Each disappeared soon after his failure. The Chief wishes you to treat his son, and hopes you can cure him, for it is a sad thing for a doctor to disappear. The curing societies say that they can do nothing for the boy."

I glanced at the women; they looked really frightened. Evidently they understood something of the language of these Canoe Portage People, or Cayugas. Even Moonhakee looked worried.

"But I am not a doctor," I found voice at last. "I know nothing about curing people." Through Many-Tongues the reply came back:

"The chief does not believe you; but if what you say is true he is sorry for you. You will begin to doctor the boy tonight. The chief will provide whatever you need if you will let him know in time to get it."

"What in the world shall I do?" I said, partly to myself and partly to Many-Tongues as our guides led us to seats on one side of the council house.

"Better ask some older person, not me," he replied. "Why don't you talk it over with your mother? What do you have a mother for, anyhow? I'll interpret."

When we explained matters to Carrying-Woman, she was more worried than ever, as she had only understood part of what had been said.

"I don't know much about such things," she said. "But if I were doing it, I would ask to see the child right away. I would look him over and try to find out what is wrong."

At my request the chief sent for the patient; the little boy looked thin and miserable. His right shoulder was swollen and his right arm was much thinner than the other. I stepped up and examined him carefully; the arm looked as if it were hung wrong, somehow; and when I touched the shoulder the child shrunk away from pain.

I made a sudden decision. "We might as well have it over with," I said. "Tell the chief I will doctor his son right now if he will give me some tobacco." After this was brought I walked over to one of the fire pits where coals were smouldering; the boy and my friends followed. Kneeling, I began to throw in little pinches of tobacco as I had been taught in Lenape land.

"Listen," I prayed as the smoke rose white. "Ye who have promised to help me, come now and show me how to cure this child." Twelve pinches I threw, and waited; then in my mind a picture took form. Ants were hurrying to and fro; then a crippled ant appeared; one of its legs was hanging limp. Another ant caught it up in its jaws and pulled hard—then the cripple was well again. Now the picture shifted to the village in England where I was born, to our town barber who knew something of doctoring, and to a lad whose arm had hung down in just the same way. The barber gave the arm a strong pull with a little twist and it was well again; I remembered just how he grasped that arm.

Beckoning to my companions as I rose, I led the boy back to where his father sat and gently laid him on his left side. Carrying-Woman and Among-the-Blossoms held him down. I grasped the arm firmly; then gave it a strong pull with a sort of twist. Something in the shoulder snapped; the child shrieked with pain and began to cry; his father sprang up angrily. It was a breathless moment; had I succeeded or failed?

Now my patient was scrambling to his feet; his crying stopped as he discovered he could now move his arm a little. He ran to show his father.

"Tell the chief," I said as calmly as I could, remembering the case of the boy in England, "that the arm will be thin for some time, but it will gradually fill out and his son will get the full use of it. The shoulder, too, will be sore for a while." We stood there, the four of us, with Moonhakee, waiting for what might come next. The chief stood staring at us, with his arm about his son. After a while he spoke, and Many-Tongues translated:

"The runner spoke the truth; you are a good doctor. What do you wish as a reward? Anything I have is yours if you desire it."

I did some quick thinking.

"I am asking for six things," I said, "one thing for every finger of this hand which cured your son, and one for the hand itself."

"You shall have them. What are they?"

"First of all I want a pretty shell bead necklace for my mother; second, a nice new dress for—for this girl. Third, I want a good bow and quiver of arrows for this boy who speaks for me. Fourth, a deerskin robe for myself. Fifth, your promise that you will not ask me to doctor anyone else in this village; and sixth, your honest answer to a question I am about to ask you."

The chief pondered. Carrying-Woman whispered and the boy interpreted: "For a while there she was sorry she let that rascal at the door take her axe!"

Many-Tongues told me afterward that I looked quite important except that my ears got so red when I spoke of "this girl" that he thought they would set fire to my scalp lock.

Now the chief answered:

"The first four things will be easy; the fifth is granted, but I am sorry, because there are a number of people here who need doctoring. As for the sixth, your question, I shall answer it truly, if I can answer it at all. What is it?"

"I am looking for a young Lenape hostage named Little-Bear," I said, and the boy interpreted. "I have been told that he is being held in one of the Five Nations villages. Where is he?"

"I cannot tell," replied the chief. "I have never even heard of Little-Bear. But they claim that all the Lenape hostages were taken to the western villages of the Big Mountain People—as far away as possible from their home country."

I had learned enough Iroquois by this time to say *"Nee-yah-weh'-ha"* for "Thank you," understood by all the five tribes. We were headed in the right direction, at least.

Our guides escorted us back to the side bench. After giving some directions, the chief, leading his son by the hand, came over to speak to us.

"Wait here," he said, "until I send you the things you asked for. If you can stay in this village a few days, we will get up a big feast and pleasure dance in your honor; but I must know now so I can talk it over with the other chiefs and the matrons."

At first I was tempted to stay; but I feared above all that I might be called upon to treat another patient —and this time it might not turn out so well. So through Many-Tongues I thanked him, but explained that we must be traveling on, as soon as possible. The chief went out, his companions followed. In a few minutes we found ourselves alone in the council house.

Carrying-Woman, sitting beside me, slipped her arm around my waist and spoke affectionately, and the boy translated.

"Son, I am proud of you. My husband thought I was foolish to adopt you, and that I would be sorry, but now I know he was wrong."

On my other side, Among-the-Blossoms spoke up. Many-Tongues laughed.

"The girl says she is proud of you, too, with good reason. After all, she says, your adoption was her idea in the beginning.

"Now that's over," Many-Tongues went on, "I'd like to say a few words for myself. I am mad at you; you have been fooling me all along. Why didn't you tell me you were a doctor?" The little fellow was half in earnest.

"I am not a doctor," I protested.

"You cured that child," he argued.

"Well, if I am a doctor, I didn't know it before. You say the chief got the idea from a runner. I do not understand that part."

"Yes, the runner described all of us, even the dog,

so there would be no mistake." Among-the-Blossoms
asked him something then, and the two talked together
in Onondaga.

Finally the boy turned to me.

"The girl thinks Tadoda'ho filled the runner full of
lies the way you'd pour corn into a sack; then sent him
here to make trouble for us, knowing that the chief would
get rid of any doctor who failed to cure his child. She
wants to know also, how you knew the way to cure, if
you are not a doctor."

"I prayed to my dream helpers," I explained. "And
they brought me the cure out of my past life."

Just then three women marched into the council
house with big wooden bowls of steaming venison stew
for each of us, a bark tray of boiled corn bread, and a
bone for Moonhakee. It was just as well this interrup-
tion came, for according to Indian belief it would not
have been proper to reveal just what had appeared in
my dream, or who my helpers were.

Before we had finished eating, a messenger came
from the chief with a nice robe for me and a long bow
and quiver of arrows for Many-Tongues. The bow was
much like the Lenape style, between four and five feet
long, and almost straight when unstrung; the string was
made of twisted strips of woodchuck hide; the quiver a
plain sack made of extra thick deerskin, with a shoulder
strap. I looked at some of the arrows curiously. They
were not very different from my own except that the
points were all slim triangles of flint, without the stems
seen on Lenape hunting arrowheads, stems so convenient
when you lash the point to the shaft with shreds of sinew.

There was also a very nice necklace made of small oval ocean shells with holes for stringing, as good as anything of the kind I had ever seen in Lenape land. This I hung about my new mother's neck with great pleasure.

But where was the girl's dress? I was beginning to worry when who should appear but my patient, the chief's little son—and I noticed he was moving his arm a little better already.

He was bearing a bundle which he managed to lay in Among-the-Blossoms' lap, then shyly withdrew. She hastened to open it. As I expected, it was a complete costume—skirt, leggings and waist, prettily embroidered with dyed deer hair and almost new. It was made almost exactly like a Lenape dress, the skirt a flat blanket-like piece worn wrapped around the body and held in place with a belt; the blouse an oblong flat piece with a hole in the middle for the head. Only the leggings were really different, having the seams up the front instead of at the side; and the embroidered designs showed many curved lines instead of the Lenape straight lines, squares and angles.

Among-the-Blossoms' eyes were shining and her smile bright when she thanked me—*"Nee-yah-weh'-ha,"* to which I now knew enough to answer *"Nyoh,"* which means "So be it."

VI.   A GOBLIN ENEMY

With the chief's permission we spent the night in the council house; and again in the morning the women brought us a satisfying meal. Then one of our guides of the evening before came with the news that he had been delegated to take us across the lake in a canoe; which, he said, would save us a great deal of walking on our trip west.

As we were leaving the village, I said to Many-Tongues:

"Do you notice that all the houses toward the lake are smaller and poorer? I wonder why that is?"

He spoke to our guide, and his reply was certainly unexpected.

"These are the houses of the Cat Nation captives whom our warriors brought in from the west a few years ago. They have all been adopted now, and speak our language, but they have never learned to build houses as good as ours." Evidently these Iroquois adopted captives in a body as well as singly. The Cat Nation are also called Eries, by the English.

We helped our guide carry down his canoe and launch it in the lake; it was made of elm bark sewn together and caulked with shredded fiber mixed with pine pitch, and strengthened inside with slim, limber poles, very much like some canoes I had seen in Lenape land. While he was paddling across, he explained that the main trail skirted the lake to its north end and then followed the outlet some distance north before reaching a suitable fording place and turning west once more; whereas this way we could travel almost straight west and pick up the main trail again later on.

When we landed, he pointed out a path which we followed west until we reached a river which Many-Tongues called the *Sway'-geh* and then we walked along its south bank for some distance beside rushing rapids or waterfalls. Noticing that the north bank seemed easier for traveling we found a fording place and crossed it— and ran right into our main east-west trail again.

The sky was cloudless; it began to get very warm as the morning wore on; by midday we were both hot and hungry, but we kept on going in order to reach the regular stopping place, which we knew would not be far away. We had learned that on this trail they lay about half a day's journey apart.

Finally we came upon a lovely spring flowing out from under some mossy rocks beneath a huge tree. This we decided must be the right place for many traces of former cooking fires and other signs lay scattered about the little glade.

Many-Tongues and I lay back luxuriously on the moss while the women rummaged in their packs for food.

"Look!" suddenly cried Many-Tongues. "There's a big hum house right over our heads." I looked: there hung a huge gray wasps' nest. At that very instant an arrow flicked through the air and buried itself in the nest.

The next moment we were stumbling through the brush pursued by hundreds of angry insects. At the same time a crazy cackling laugh filled the air and someone unseen pelted us with stones. At this my new mother charged back toward the nest, brandishing her axe, but could find nobody. The rest of us ran until Among-the-Blossoms tripped over a root and fell flat, sobbing. I was trying to help her up when Many-Tongues came along.

"She says it's no use," he told me. "She can't run any farther." He was half-crying himself. Although no more wasps seemed to be following us, we picked seven off the girl that were still walking about on her clothing, looking for a place to sting. I had four on me and Many-Tongues five, and one was still clinging to Moonhakee.

Carrying-Woman came up then, and the three of us helped Among-the-Blossoms to her feet and escorted her to a shady spot. Then I noticed she had been stung several times in the face and one eye was almost closed.

This angered me beyond words. I remembered how those eyes had looked into mine as I hung on the torture frame. How could I forget?

"If I could catch that vile sneak who let fly that arrow," I said, "he'd never shoot another. I'd beat his brains out!"

"You could not do that," said Many-Tongues. "No

human person ever played that trick on us—that was *Jee-gah-eh-heh'-wa,* a Stone-Roller goblin."

"Why would a goblin need to use an arrow?" I argued. "I think it was a man, and I am going back there to find out who it was. Besides, I am hungry and all our food is there."

When Many-Tongues interpreted this, Carrying-Woman spoke earnestly, looking at me.

"Your mother says better not go now or the flying stingers will get after you again. She says wait until about dark when they have all gone to bed."

We waited until late that afternoon to please her, and then I did a little scouting. Cautiously approaching the place, I found our belongings scattered about, but no wasps in sight. I looked then for the nest—but no hum house. It was gone! I confess I began to think of goblins then.

I called the others, and while the two women started to get out the food, Many-Tongues and I searched for clues. The only thing we found was a sort of plug made from shredded bark fiber, and we were trying to figure this out when there came a wail from the girl.

"All our food has been ruined; we have nothing to eat!" We looked; somebody had mixed our parched corn with dirt; our shelled corn was gone altogether; all our dried meat and corn bread had been smeared with something that smelled terrible.

Many-Tongues, sniffing, thought it must be some stuff taken from the beaver which is used to scent traps to attract fur-bearing animals. Trappers usually carry it, he said, in little bottles made of bone or deer horn.

"I tell you what I think," I said. "This was done

by a man, who brought the big wasp nest here with its
doorways all plugged up with fiber like we found. He
thought we would stop here because everybody does. He
hung up the nest and pulled the plugs so they would fall
out at the slightest jar. When the right time came, he
shot the arrow, the plugs fell out, and you know the rest.
He must have protected himself in some way from the
wasps when he spoiled our food and took away the nest."

Many-Tongues interpreted this to the women; then
Among-the-Blossoms spoke up and the boy said:

"This girl thinks you may be right. She wonders if
she looks as funny to you with her face all swelled up
as you look to her. 'Something like a lop-sided pumpkin,' she says, 'that's the way you look!'" At this she gave
me a one-sided smile, and we all laughed. The disaster
had its funny side.

Then Carrying-Woman said something, in very sad
tones.

"She says," interpreted Many-Tongues, "that she
noticed some berry bushes quite a ways back along the
trail, and we had better hurry back there and pick some
before dark. That's all the supper we'll have, she tells
us."

That night we camped on a rough bare rocky hilltop, with Many-Tongues and me taking turns at standing guard for fear of a sneak attack. About dawn I ventured out hunting and was lucky enough to get a deer
before the sun was above the treetops. I was greatly relieved when I returned to camp and found my companions safe.

While the women were packing their carrying

frames after our breakfast (which was entirely of venison), Carrying-Woman was talking to Many-Tongues. He turned to me.

"Your mother says we should make camp somewhere and stay long enough for you to kill a few more deer, so we can dry the meat for us to eat on the road, and tan the skins so we will have something to trade for corn at the next town. She says you should find a good place as soon as you can before this meat spoils."

I was puzzled, for open spaces convenient to water were hard to find in this heavily-wooded country, and we needed freedom from trees and brush that might give shelter to an approaching enemy. I looked in vain for such a place until late in the morning, when we suddenly came out of the forest upon the north end of another big lake; this time on the west side of its outlet—which was the *Sway'-geh* River we had been following. The trail turned west along the beach, then south along the western shore of the lake for some distance, then turned squarely off into the forest. We continued south keeping to the beach however, because I thought I could see a safe camping place. Sure enough, there was a low point jutting out into the lake, treeless and without a bush on it more than knee high. It was exactly what we wanted.

As we walked out on the point Many-Tongues indicated a dark mass of clouds gathering in the west.

"It is going to rain again before night," he warned. "We must work fast to get our camp built in time."

We all laid down our burdens with sighs of relief; then we started in. The first thing was to cut some poles to make a drying rack for the meat. That is not as easy as it sounds, for we had no steel axe, and Carrying-Woman's stone axe was rather slow. To speed up the pole cutting, while she was busy, Many-Tongues and I worked together. I would climb a sapling, bending it over; then while he held it down, I sawed across the stretched fibers at the bend with my flint knife.

If there had been time, I would have found some flinty pebble and chipped it into a rough blade which would have sawed just as well, and spared my beautiful knife, which Among-the-Blossoms might have used on the meat. As it was she had to cut the venison into strips with flint flakes, while the rest of us were pole cutting. Then we had to gather wood to make the smoke which would cure the meat and keep away the flies. And finally, with an eye on the gathering clouds, we built a little roof of bark over the drying rack.

The shelter for ourselves was next; we cut two stout forked poles each standing about six feet high; a ten-foot ridgepole to lay across them; and eight poles, twelve feet long for rafters to make a shed roof on one side of our ridge. These we covered with sheets of bark from some basswood trees that we had noticed near a stream running into the lake. We were just tying down the last thin poles to hold this bark in place when the rain started. And we had to rush to get in a supply of dry cooking wood, all four of us working together.

It was not until just before nightfall that the women could find time to broil a few strips of venison for our supper. We had eaten nothing since early morning. All night long Many-Tongues and I took turns watching.

At one time I thought I heard someone walking, and

Moonhakee growled. I woke the boy, but we could see nothing in the rain and the darkness. I doubt if any prowler could have seen us from the land side, for our shed faced east, toward the lake, and our drying frame was directly in front of it. Therefore all view of its low fire was cut off.

We had just about made up our minds that it was a false alarm, when a weird song sounded from across the waters, the wildest and strangest I had ever heard. It was loud enough to wake Carrying-Woman and the girl from their well-earned rest. We sat shivering and listened; first it seemed to be out of the water, then out of our side of the lake; again it seemed to come from no place in particular. The air was full of it. Moonhakee crawled as far back under the shed as he could squeeze himself and refused to come out. The song or songs never stopped until daylight.

"That was the Dark Dance music of the Stone-Roller goblins," Carrying-Woman informed us. And then she did a strange thing—she pared the finger and toe nails of all of us with a sharp flint flake, and tied the trimmings up in a bit of buckskin.

"*Sah'-yenh geh, neh oh-yen'-gwah?*" she asked, meaning, "Have you any tobacco?"

I had a small packet in a shoulder pouch, and this I gave her; she took both packets and put them under a flat stone on the lake shore not far from our camp. Many-Tongues whispered that it was an offering to the Stone-Rollers who are said to like tobacco and use human nail parings for medicine.

Next day was rainy, but we did go out to see whether

the offerings had been taken. The stone had been turned over and the packets were gone. In the mud nearby was a single small track—like the footprint of a crippled child, blurred by the rain, but unmistakable. We shivered as we scurried back to our shed.

"We'll hear no more songs," Carrying-Woman predicted.

Later in the day we quieted down enough to enjoy a few good naps to make up for last night; and between them I spent my time in a very pleasant way, making a real start at learning the Onondaga language. The first and most useful sentence I learned was *"Hoht nen'-geh gah-yah'-jee?"* meaning "What is this, its name?"—in other words, "What is the name of this?"

Soon I learned the name of almost every article in our camp, such as kettle, knife, moccasin, also some animals and such things as "I like," "I don't like," "Come here," "Take it," "It is good." By evening I could say "Give me the water," so my companions could understand me. Only I said it awkwardly, word by word *"Dus'-hah-wah neh oh-nay'-gah-nos,"* whereas I should have combined *dus'-hah-wah,* the word for "give-me" with *oh-nay'-gah-nos,* meaning water, and made it *"Dus-nay-gah'-hwah"*—a whole sentence in one word. Anyhow, my three companions were delighted. Now I could understand a little, at least, of what they said; and from that time on my knowledge of the language grew rapidly.

Three more deer I brought in during the days that followed, of which the women dried the meat and tanned the skins, while Many-Tongues and I helped all they would let us. I noticed that they saved all the deer hoofs, and I found out why later.

Skin-tanning is a wretchedly messy business, with plenty of hard work. Each skin had to be stretched on a pole frame to which it was lashed by thongs run through holes punched around the edges. Then the busy workers removed every bit of fat and tissue from the flesh side with stone scrapers.

The skin after being taken off the frame was soaked in water, rolled up and put away in the shade until the hair loosened. At this stage I found two smooth logs on the beach; over which the two tanners laid the skins while they scraped off the hair with tools made from a deer's leg bones. Next they worked a nasty mess of deer brains, saved for the purpose, into the skins; finally stretching them again and working them with a wedge-shaped tool of wood until they were dry and beautifully soft. Smoking was the finishing touch; the women stitched the four skins roughly together forming a tent, which was suspended over a hole in the ground containing a low fire of rotten wood.

Every night the boy and I took turns guarding the camp; but there were no more midnight alarms nor weird songs. However we never were really at ease; we felt as if someone were always watching us, whether goblins or humans we did not know. Both the women said, "Goblins."

I ground some fishhooks out of pieces of deer bone as I had been taught in Lenape land. First you shape out a flat oval blank of deer bone by sawing and scraping with flint, and grinding with sandstone; the blank should be about an inch and a half long and about half that width. Then you cut the middle out of this by grooving round and round with a sharp flint point, from both sides. The thin band of bone remaining will make two hooks, which, of course, must be sharpened on sandstone and notched for the line.

Among-the-Blossoms gave me some fiber twine from a ball her mother had made for her, and we went fishing. By the time we moved on we were as tired of bony little fish as we were of nothing but venison and a few berries.

One day the girl asked me to bore little holes through the pointed toes of all of her deer hoofs—which I did with a small flint drill I always carried with my tools in one of my shoulder pouches; then she strung each one on a thin deerskin thong a few inches long. These were all brought together into a single knot; it must have been some sort of a rattle, but there were too many hoofs for a hand rattle, or a knee rattle for dancers, and she would not tell me what it was. "Wait and see," was all she would say.

Just at dusk she crept out and stretched several strands of her mother's fiber cord across the point, between us and the shore, a little way above the ground, fastening the ends to low shrubs growing at the water's edge. In one place there was no bush, so she drove a short stick into the ground to support the string.

From each of the original strands the girl ran strings which came together at one end of our shed, and here she tied the bunch of deer hoofs.

"Now we can sleep," said Among-the-Blossoms,

"*Ees oh'-nih.*" She looked at me, and smiled when she saw I understood. The words mean "You also." It was plain that no one could approach our camp at night without tripping over one of the strings; then the deer-hoofs would rattle loudly; Moonhakee would bark, we would all awaken.

"But what if they come by water?" I asked.

Among-the-Blossoms had not thought of that, and I could see she was ready to cry; after all her planning and work the problem was not solved after all. Signalling the boy to keep silent, in my broken Onondaga I explained that it was very good to have the land side protected anyhow; now we would only have to watch the water.

Some time in the night, while I was on guard, the deer hoofs did rattle, waking my companions, and we heard something running away in the darkness. Moonhakee barked, but did not pursue. Later on, when the others had gone back to bed, I saw a black thing out on the lake, dimly visible in the starlight, gradually approaching our camp. I shot an arrow at it, and it beat a splashing retreat, finally disappearing into the shadow of the hills across the lake.

The deer-hoof alarm may have been sounded by a prowling wolf looking for bones; the thing in the water may have been one of the strange giant deer sometimes seen in these parts, which are now called "moose." I know they like to wade in lakes and eat water lilies. Whatever it was we did not worry about it; we gladly moved away next day, taking to the trail again, supplied with plenty of dried meat, and with four good soft-tanned buckskins to trade for corn.

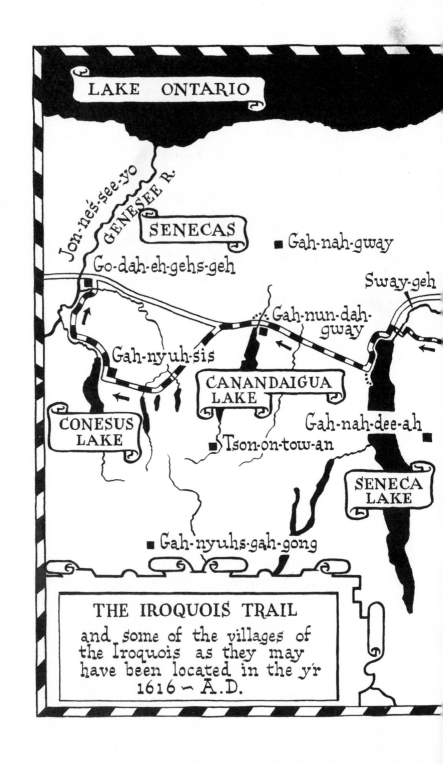

LAKE ONTARIO

Jon-neś-see-yo
GENESEE R.

SENECAS

■ Gah-nah-gway

Sway-geh

Go-dah-eh-gehs-geh

Gah-nun-dah-gway

Gah-nyuh-sis

CANANDAIGUA LAKE

Gah-nah-dee-ah

CONESUS LAKE

■ Tson-on-tow-an

SENECA LAKE

■ Gah-nyuhs-gah-gong

THE IROQUOIS TRAIL
and some of the villages of
the Iroquois as they may
have been located in the yr
1616 — A.D.

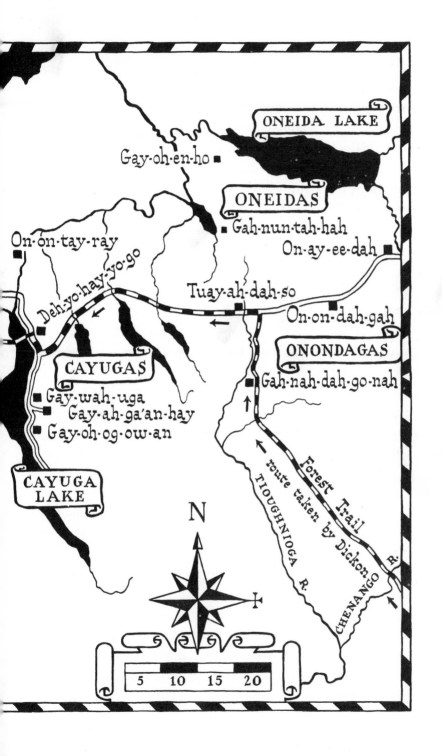

We went north along the lake shore to the main trail and then turned west again; about midday we crossed a fair-sized creek. Some two or three leagues farther on I noticed that Among-the-Blossoms was becoming very tired, although she would not complain. I suggested that we camp on the shady banks of a little brook. While she got the supper things ready, Carrying-Woman gathered some wood and built a little fire. In the meantime Many-Tongues went out with his bow and arrows to look for a rabbit to give us fresh meat for our evening meal.

When the sun sank low and he had not returned, we began to worry. Should I leave the women alone long enough to search for him? I was trying to decide, when we heard somebody scream. The boy's voice—he was screaming for help! Forgetting danger we rushed in the direction of the sound.

The boy was hanging by one leg from a tree limb, head down, his head encased in a deerskin sack crudely painted to represent a human skull; his hands tied behind him. The hideous mask had breathing holes and mouth hole, but no eye holes.

We cut him down, pulled the sack off his head, loosed his bonds. The boy seemed uninjured, but so exhausted he could hardly speak. Only then did we have sense enough to look around for enemies—none were in sight. Even so it was lucky we thought to bring our weapons: Among-the-Blossoms had my war club, I my bow and arrows, and, of course, Carrying-Woman her axe. I am sure they would have been gone when we returned to our campground, if we had left them lying there.

We half led, half carried the boy back, Moonhakee running ahead.

"*Saht-gaht'-toh!*—Look!" whispered Among-the-Blossoms. "Look at the dog! He's sniffing of our bedding —and growling!"

The faithful Moonhakee had caught the scent of evil. Someone had evidently untied the bundle of robes that Many-Tongues had been carrying; now I found a long stick and unrolled them, wondering what could be inside. Carrying-Woman stood by with her axe, and it is a good thing she did. From down in the center of the bundle two big rattlesnakes came slithering out—coiled ready to strike! After Mother chopped the head off one with her axe and I smashed the other with a rock, I found proof that they had not hidden in our bundle of robes of their own accord, but had been placed there. Their rattles were thickly coated with pine pitch which muffled their warning sound!

Many-Tongues told us that someone had sneaked up behind him and thrown a robe over his head, nearly smothering him. Then they had tied his hands behind his back, stuck something in his mouth so he could not make a sound, pulled the sack over his head; finally hanging him up by one foot and pulling out the gag so he could yell.

"Was it Stone-Roller goblins?" asked Carrying-Woman anxiously.

"I don't know; couldn't see them," was the response. "It felt like four or five full-sized men. I wouldn't mind it so much if they had not taken my new bow and arrows," he added bitterly.

"We must find some way to stop this," I said. "The other things have been more like cruel jokes, although the doctor trick might have been dangerous. But rattlesnakes are deadly. If Moonhakee had not been here, Among-the-Blossoms would have opened the bundle; she usually does, and one of those snakes might have bitten her!"

"Why do you think of me?" she asked. "Any one of us might have been bitten. Just the same I like it when you think of me!" She flashed me one of her pretty smiles.

After we ate our scanty supper of toasted dried venison, we held a council of war—in whispers for fear of being overhead. Next day we put our plan into effect.

The sun was halfway up the sky when we reached a patch of very stony ground where the forest and undergrowth were thinner, and finding a suitable spot we turned quickly off the beaten path, taking care to leave no sign, and hid ourselves in a patch of brush where we could watch the trail. If our enemy were following, we would surely see him—or them—we thought.

Hardly were we settled when a stone came sailing through the air and struck the ground at my side, and we heard again that blood-chilling, cackling laugh. I rushed in what I thought was the direction of the laugh; but stopped after fifty paces or so, and, luckily, looked back. Just in time to glimpse someone sneaking up on the bush where I had left my companions. I quickly scouted around until I could get a good view: Big-Nose, Tado-da'ho's servant!

I took quick aim and let an arrow fly; the dwarf screamed hoarsely, seemed to stumble, fell heavily; then rose and rushed off into the forest. I ran to the place where he fell; arrows had spilled out of his quiver and I recognized some of them as Many-Tongues'. No doubt, this was the creature who had placed the snakes in our bedding. No goblin; just a warped and evil-minded human, acting under Tadoda'ho's orders.

We pushed on then to reach, before anything else happened, the first town of the Big Mountain People, now called Senecas by the English. Its name, Many-Tongues said, was *Gah-nun-dah'-gway* or "Town-Selected" and it stood on a terrace overlooking the outlet of still another lake; smaller, but even more beautiful than the others I had seen. This whole Iroquois country seems to be full of long, narrow lakes, great and small, mostly running north and south with outlets at the north end.

As we came down a steep slope, we first saw "Town-Selected" sitting in the midst of its wide-spread corn fields, its clustered cabins and long-houses surrounded by a substantial palisade of logs, with the bright waters of the lake beyond. Smoke was rising from cooking fires. It looked like a haven of refuge for tired and hungry wanderers like us.

We approached the town openly and happily, thinking of rest and refreshment and the chance to trade our buckskins for the corn which would make a welcome change in our food; and I especially, hoped to get news, or perhaps even to find Little-Bear himself.

Suddenly six or eight armed warriors stepped out and blocked our path; their leader spoke a few words.

"They won't let us come into the village; they know all about us, he says," Many-Tongues groaned.

"Tell him we will do no harm; all we wish to do is to trade some tanned buckskins for corn to eat."

The boy spoke in this strange dialect; the grim-looking leader of the guard growled something in reply, gripped his big war club menacingly.

"He says they will not trade with us; we had better go away or we shall get hurt."

Drearily we circled the town to the north, waded the outlet of the lake; dismally and silently we made camp in the brush a little way off the trail, which here again ran along the beach.

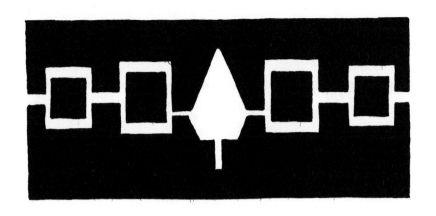

VII. A MESSENGER OF SHAME

Carrying-Woman handed a piece of dried meat to each one of us; it tasted like so much bark, we were so tired of it.

"This is all the supper we'll get," she said. *"Ah-geh'* I thought we would be eating corn soup by this time!" She chewed thoughtfully a few minutes. "You know," she continued, "It looks as if Tadoda'ho must have sent another runner to this village with a sack full of lies to make trouble for us."

"I wish I knew just what is the matter," I put in. "Then we could plan what to do. And I wanted, above all, to ask here about Little-Bear."

"And I wish," said Among-the-Blossoms, "that we could trade off these buckskins. While we were tanning them, I was thinking of the corn they would bring and all the delicious dishes we could make from it."

Many-Tongues scratched his head.

"Maybe I could sneak into the village," he said. "You see, I speak the language, and . . ."

I interrupted him. "That would be too dangerous. Someone who had seen you with us might recognize you."

"A plan has come to me." Carrying-Woman murmured, "We might dress up Many-Tongues like a girl; then nobody would recognize him!"

"I don't think I want to go after all," the boy growled.

I pretended to examine his ears. "Hoh-hoh!" I chortled. "What makes your ears so red, my little friend?" He looked at the ground and said nothing.

"In truth we can continue to get along without corn," Carrying-Woman went on, looking sadly at the empty clay kettles. "But it may be a long trail to the next town; and when we get there, Tadoda'ho's runner may have arrived first."

Still looking at the ground, Many-Tongues muttered something.

"What did you say?" Among-the-Blossoms asked.

"I said I would go! Must I yell it out loud?"

The women sacrificed one of our large buckskins to make the skirt; the waist or cape was cut from a small skin that had been brought along for mending material. Girls that age did not wear leggings except in cold weather, so they were spared that trouble. Finally they rubbed the garments, especially the fresh cuts, with dirt to give them the look of long use. When Many-Tongues was dressed, they brushed his hair smoothly and gathered it into one braid down his back; finally hanging around his neck a string of my new mother's beads.

"*Gweh!*" I exclaimed. "You make a sweet *ik-sa-goh'-nah* maiden!"

"What will you say," Among-the-Blossoms teased, "if some nice young man asks you to marry him?"

"No more talk from you two!" The boy picked up the remaining skins, rolled them into as small a package as possible, then disappeared up the trail in the gathering dusk.

Among-the-Blossoms sat down suddenly upon a log, saying something in Onondaga I did not catch; but I could see she was worried about Many-Tongues. Carrying-Woman busied herself unrolling our robes, axe in hand in case of more rattlesnakes.

Now the moon came up, big and bright, from behind the hill upon which the town stood, flooding woodland and lake with its magic. The first thing I knew I discovered Among-the-Blossoms' head on my shoulder, and my arm somehow found its way around her waist. White-Deer was not the only wonderful girl in the world! I am sure Carrying-Woman noticed this, because she kept away from us, busily cleaning up the spots of ground we had selected to sleep on, picking up every little stick and pebble. How long this might have gone on, I do not know; because a short-skirted figure suddenly appeared bearing a sack.

"*Nay'toh,*" said Many-Tongues' voice. "Here's all the corn we can carry. Take it and unbraid my hair, won't you?"

When Carrying-Woman had done this, and folded away his disguise in her pack, the boy told his story.

"I went into town with some travelers coming from

the west," he said. "You must have heard them passing right after I left. It was getting dark, but I looked around and found an old woman trying to carry a lot of firewood. I helped her with it; she lived in a cabin, not a long-house; then she asked me in and gave me a big bowl of corn soup. *Gweh!* It was *do-gehs' oh-yah'-neh,* truly fine, and I thought of you all while I was eating it." He chuckled saucily. "Grandma has nobody to hunt for her but her garden is doing well and she was glad to trade corn for the skins."

"Did you find out why they would not let us into the village?" I asked.

"Yes, your mother's right. It was a runner from Tadoda'ho who told the chiefs a lot of lies—about you especially. He said you were a scout for a very dangerous tribe of people who would one day cheat the Long-House Builders out of all their possessions, if they let you get a start. That is why they would not let us in or trade with us."

"How did you find that out?" I questioned, feeling rather queer when I thought of the actions of the English toward the Indians at Jamestown.

"*Ah-geh'!* I had to tell a lot of lies myself. I told Grandma that I lived in a small village to the west and that my aunt, who was sick, had sent me in to trade the skins; and I asked her if anything had happened lately in the big town. And then she told me all about the runner from Tadoda'ho, and how we had been turned away this afternoon. I felt ashamed," he continued, looking at the ground, "when she called me 'daughter' and asked me to be sure to come to see her whenever I was in town."

"Did you get any news of Little-Bear?" I asked.

"No, I could not think of any way to ask about him without making her suspect something."

When morning came, Carrying-Woman parched some of the corn in the hot ashes, which she sifted out with a little basket sieve she carried in her pack; then she ground the parched corn between two stones and made us some hot mush in our clay kettle. Even without tree sugar or grease it was wonderful.

Breakfast finished we again turned our faces west, but not for long. We had hardly left the lake shore when the trail forked; one branch, the most traveled, turning northwest the other southwest.

"Which way shall we go?" I asked Many-Tongues.

"I don't know," the boy replied. "I have never been this far west; but they say there are Big Mountain villages in both directions."

"The right hand fork looks like the main trail," said Among-the-Blossoms. "If Tadoda'ho sends another runner to tell lies about us, he will think we went that way. Let's take the left fork."

I must admit it, the more I saw of Among-the-Blossoms, the more I liked her. As I had done in the case of White-Deer, I tried to fight off this feeling; for I knew, if we discovered that Little-Bear was dead, I must return to Turtle-Town and White-Deer would be waiting. But I could not forget that it was Among-the-Blossoms who had saved my life.

And so we marched southwest quite happily; the weather was fine, we had plenty of food; at this rate we would soon reach the western villages where Little-Bear was supposed to be. During the forenoon we crossed a large creek or small river running north and in the afternoon passed a pretty lake, long and narrow like the rest, but very much smaller.

The sun was low when we sighted still another little lake to the south as we crossed a hill. It lay some distance from the trail, but we decided to pass the night there, under the evergreen trees which surrounded it. We took no particular care about our camp, nor did we stand guard, for we really imagined our troubles with the dwarf were over. Foolishly I thought my arrow had killed him, or wounded him so badly that he would not trouble us again.

Next morning came the crowning disaster. We had eaten our breakfast, and everything was packed to leave, when we missed Moonhakee; we called and called in vain. Suddenly we heard him shrieking with pain some distance away.

"It may be a trap like that other time," Many-Tongues warned.

"Don't leave anything behind," Carrying-Woman added, "or Big-Nose will put poison in it."

So, carrying our belongings, we hurried to Moonhakee's rescue. As I had half expected, there hung the poor dog, dangling from a tree by one hind leg. I ran to cut him down; tripped and fell heavily, heard Among-the-Blossoms scream; then something struck me a terrible blow and I knew no more.

The first thing I remember was an awful headache and backache; then I found my legs were just one mass of pains and aches; I could not move them. I heard a soft familiar voice say in Onondaga, "Take a little water," and a firm hand raised my head so I could drink. As my eyesight cleared, the first things I saw were the two women's anxious faces; then Many-Tongues looking pale and scared enough. And there, sure enough, was Moon-hakee, apparently none the worse for his adventure. What had happened, anyhow?

Among-the-Blossoms read the question in my eyes before I was able to speak, and explained as well as she could in simple Onondaga with Many-Tongues to help out when I did not understand.

"*Nee-yah-weh'-ha.* I am thankful," she said. "I was afraid we had lost you forever. It was a trap, but different from what we had expected. Moonhakee was the bait. When you tripped over the rope, a lot of big stones came down from the tree overhead. You fell forward quite a way, more than Big-Nose had expected, I think, and most of the stones hit your legs. One struck Many-Tongues, too. His arm may be broken; he says he can't use it."

"Wha-what shall we do? I-I-can't walk," I lamented.

"We will make a litter to carry you on, dear Son," said Mother. "Yes, we'll get you to the next town, never fear."

So I lay in the shade, trying to keep from groaning, while Many-Tongues sat dejectedly by, his right arm hanging helpless, and the women trotted to and fro with axe and knife, gathering poles and strips of bark for my litter.

I worried so much about the danger of the dwarf's following up his success with another attack that Carry-

ing-Woman sat me up against the tree trunk with bow
and arrows in hand. I was so sure that he would return,
at least to see how well his trap had done its work, that
I told the boy we must keep silent and watch.

It was Many-Tongues' keen eye that sighted Big-
Nose peering from the bushes; he nudged me, then I
saw the dwarf and let fly an arrow. It drew a yell of
pain and a torrent of words I did not catch.

"He says," the boy interpreted, "that you have
wounded his bow arm once too often. Next time, he
claims, he will kill all four of us, also the dog."

"*Sen-dah-no'-gehs!* You lie!" I shouted. I was glad
I had learned the word. Then the women came in with
the last of the needed materials and we told them the
news.

"Big-Nose always was a liar," Carrying-Woman
said. "He is proud of it. He may be lying when he says
his bow arm is wounded, to throw us off our guard. Just
let me get at him. I'll chop his head with this axe!"

Finally the litter was built. Sometimes they carry a
wounded man slung from a single pole; but this was two
long poles with cross pieces to hold them in place, all
tied together with tough strips of inner basswood bark,
and a coarse netting of the same for me to lie on. They
laid it on the ground beside me and helped me squirm
into it, although I thought I would faint from pain.

Among-the-Blossoms picked up my bow and quiver.
"If you two will carry him," she said, "I'll be the guard.
We surely need one. There is no telling what Big-Nose
will try next."

They had attached shoulder straps to the handles of

the stretcher at both ends. Carrying-Woman knelt at my head, Many-Tongues at my feet and both adjusted the shoulder straps.

"*Hau, oh-neh'*, come, now!" she exclaimed and rose to her feet. The boy tried hard, but weakened by his injury, he could not raise my weight, and dropped to his knees again.

"*Ah-geh', hee'-yah thak-gway'-nee-ah!*" he groaned, which means "Alas, I cannot do it!"

"And one woman cannot carry Big-Turtle alone," Among-the-Blossoms added, looking about as if to find some answer to the problem. Suddenly she exclaimed, "I've got a plan—hope it works. Let me have your bow and three arrows!" She took them and disappeared into the brush, which was quite thick here. Many-Tongues had told me that she was supposed to be really expert with the bow, but I had never seen before any girl or woman with such weapons in her hands.

A few minutes anxious waiting—then we heard her talking, and a growling voice answering. When Moon-hakee heard that voice, he growled too, bristled, huddled close. Now the sounds came nearer. We watched breathlessly. Mother gripped her axe.

Suddenly Big-Nose appeared, weaponless, blood dribbling from his right arm. Behind him walked Among-the-Blossoms, bow in hand, arrow on string. On her back was another bow and quiver which must have been his. One look at his feet and I knew who had made the "Stone-Roller" tracks.

"You stand right there, Big-Nose," she commanded, handing me my bow and arrows. I managed to sit up.

"You, Big-Turtle," she went on, "shoot him if he tries to run. I am going to doctor his arm because we need him."

Mother stood twiddling her axe. "If you need him I suppose I'll have to wait," she grumbled.

Rummaging in her sewing kit the girl found a strip of tanned deerskin for a bandage and some shredded inner bark of cedar for a pad, and soon had the wound dressed.

"Now," she said to the dwarf, "you take the foot of the litter and go ahead; Carrying-Woman will take the other end, and you two will carry Big-Turtle to the next town while I guard."

"Can't," growled Big-Nose. "Arm hurts too much."

"Carry the weight by the shoulder strap," she retorted, "or would you like better one arrow between the ribs?"

Big-Nose made no reply, but adjusted the strap.

"Now I'll hide our stuff in the bushes," Among-the-Blossoms said. "We'll come back for it later."

"You don't have to," my new mother told her. "I can still carry my pack frame if you will put it on me."

"And I'll take the other," Many-Tongues added.

The girl hurriedly fixed the robe bundle so she could carry it on her back and leave her arms free, picked up the bow and arrows. We were off.

We must have made a queer picture. Mother was so tall and the dwarf so short that my litter tipped steeply. A woman litter bearer carrying also a pack frame, a boy with a pack frame; a girl guarding us with bow and arrow. What a procession!

Among-the-Blossoms was ready to shoot Big-Nose in the back if he tried any tricks, and he knew it. Moonhakee followed at a distance; it was plain he did not wish to associate with Big-Nose. Whether this was because the scent of Tadoda'ho's snakes still clung to his servant, or because the dwarf had abused Moonhakee during the time the dog was missing right after my capture, we never knew.

Several times Among-the-Blossoms called a halt for rest, but we reached the Big Mountain (Seneca) town of *Ga-nyuh'-sis* about midday. It stood on the east shore of still another small lake, not far south of the outlet. My bearers set me down in the public square, near one of the council-house doors.

"*Nee-yah-weh'-ha,*" sighed Among-the-Blossoms. "Again I am thankful."

Big-Nose stood still with his back toward us.

"Go ahead, kill me now," he growled at last. "My work is done. I wait your arrow."

"You deserve it," the girl said. "But we don't do things that way." She noticed my new mother was fingering her axe handle. "Do we, Carrying-Woman?"

"Maybe not," said Carrying-Woman, looking sadly at her pet. "But this axe is hungry for that creature's brains!"

"Mother," I said, "you sound ferocious. Has that axe ever really tasted an enemy's brains?"

"You saw what it did to that rattlesnake!" she replied with a half smile—and that was all I could get out of her.

"Let's send Big-Nose back to Onondaga with a message," I suggested. "A message to Tadoda'ho." The dwarf turned and faced us. "Are you useful to Tadoda'ho?" I asked him.

"*Do-gehs'!* Truly!" he grunted.

"You tell Tadoda'ho not to send you out to play any more tricks on us. Next time you might not come back!"

"*Nyoh!* So be it! Give me my bow and arrows!"

"No," Among-the-Blossoms said. "They belong to Many-Tongues now, because you took his. You could not hunt anyhow with that sore arm."

"I'll starve!"

"Oh no you won't," Carrying-Woman said. She rummaged in her pack and dragged out a generous portion of dried venison. "I'd rather chop your head than feed you," she grumbled, "but if son wants to do it this way—here, take this!"

It was all Big-Nose could do to get it all into his shoulder pouch. He stood there staring at us for a few minutes, his ugly mouth working as if he wanted to say something—then he turned suddenly and disappeared into the gathering crowd.

"How did you manage it?" I demanded of Among-the-Blossoms. "I think you are wonderful!"

"I think so, too!" said my new mother.

Among-the-Blossoms gave us one of her pretty smiles that brought out all her dimples.

"I happened to think of Big-Nose," she explained, "and that if he were really wounded he would be trying to doctor himself not far away, not expecting any more danger from us. In that case I would be able to take him by surprise. And that's just what I did."

"You took a big risk," I said.

"Perhaps. But we could not let you lie there suffering."

The curious crowd around my litter increased and Many-Tongues was kept busy chattering Big Mountain, Seneca language. Finally a woman who belonged to Carrying-Woman's clan, the Turtle, agreed to take us in. The woman grabbed one end of the litter, her husband the other, and we were in the Turtle long-house in a few minutes.

This long-house had no compartments, but the bunks ran in a continuous row on both sides from one end to the other, each family using as many as they needed. Naturally we were allotted adjoining bunks near those of our hosts.

While I lay on the litter, the pain was only a dull

ache, but moving me to a bunk brought it all on again,
worse than ever, and I nearly fainted, while the women
hovered over me anxiously.

All agreed that Many-Tongues and I needed a doctor; but we had nothing to offer him as a fee; that is,
nothing that could be spared. I could not give up my
war club, knife, bow and arrows. And certainly Carrying-Woman could not give up that bloodthirsty axe of
hers! And nobody would want my "dream bundle," even
if I let it go.

Our hosts talked it over with the women, with Many-
Tongues for interpreter, and finally seemed to come to
some decision, which of course I could not catch.

"Our new friends say," the boy explained, "that
there is an herb doctor in this village who might work
on you and me if our women would make something for
him. He has no womenfolk of his own and that's the way
he gets his clothes. The singing doctors, they say, charge
high fees."

The doctor came in a little later and looked us over,
feeling, twisting and hurting. He said my right leg was
broken below the knee and he would have to set it; the
rest, he claimed, was nothing but bruises except one short
deep cut, also on the right leg. The boy's hurt was only
bad bruises, he said.

Carrying-Woman held me on her lap with her
strong arms tight about me while the doctor was setting
my leg; the pain was terrific but finally the leg was set
and a bark splint put on.

The first day the women were seldom far away from
my bed, as they helped our hostess or worked on a deer-

skin shoulder pouch they had promised the doctor as a fee.

Next day, however, they had to go outside, because the long-house was too dark for fine work, and the time had come for quill embroidery. Many-Tongues had gone visiting and I was left alone, that is, with nobody I could talk to, and time dragged heavily.

My friends must have realized how hard it was for me, because they built me a bunk under an old bark shed outside, and that became home for all of us while we remained in the village of *Gah-nyuh'-sis*. The shed would barely keep rain off us, but we liked it better than the long-house.

The morning after our move, Carrying-Woman was in the long-house, helping our late hostess, and I was lying on my bunk watching Among-the-Blossoms. She was sitting there, busily embroidering and intent on her task, when I felt a chill loneliness stealing over me. Finally I called to her.

"*Gah'-jee!* Come here!"

She laid aside her awl and colored quills and rising from her mat, stepped over to my bedside.

"*Sahd-yenh'!*" I commanded. "Sit down!"

She obeyed and I hungrily clasped her hand in mine. She surveyed me critically.

"*Ot-chee'!* Horrors!" she exclaimed. "*Ah-gwahs' ut'-kee neh sgon-see'-geh!* Very much dirty thy face is!"

"*Ah-geh'!* Alas!" I lamented, in my awkward Onondaga, "*Oh-nay'-gah-nos hee-yah'-teh wahk'-yenh!* Water not I have."

Giggling, for the words were not quite correctly

Iroquois artifacts of wood: bowl, spoons, stirring paddle, and basket.

spoken, she brought water in a wooden bowl, with shredded bark for washcloth and towel, and gave me a good scrubbing. Then she produced a pretty little comb made of deer antler with the back carved to represent a wolf—she belonged to the Wolf Clan—also a brush made from a porcupine tail set in a wooden handle. With these instruments she must have extracted a lot of grass and sticks from my scalp lock, the way it felt.

Again she looked me over.

"You look better now," she said. "But there is one thing more, and you will have to do it for yourself. Hair is beginning to grow on your face; you should learn to pull it out the way our men do."

"I'll try," I replied, not liking the idea any too much. "But you will have to get me a pair of those little clam-shell pincers I see them using."

"Better see what you can do with your fingers first."

It was true—fingers were more used than pincers. Most men, as they sit talking or resting, are continually feeling of their faces; when they find a hair, they pull it out. And this is true not only of the Iroquois, but the Lenapes. As for myself I was reaching the age when I would have to pull hairs, shave, or grow a beard. I could not shave, because I had no razor; and I could not wear a beard. I knew if I did, I would lose my standing as a human being in the eyes of my Iroquois friends. They would regard me as some kind of fur-bearing animal! Their own beards, when they do let them grow, are very thin—quite different from an Englishman's.

"I want to tell you," Among-the-Blossoms went on,

"that I think you are *do-gehs' oh-yah'-neh* too. But I really was mad at you once."

"When was that?"

"That first day on the trail, when you and Many-Tongues were talking all the time in a language I could not understand."

"I remember now. We were talking about the Five Nations Peace League. What a wonderful thing that is!"

"Truly it is great," she agreed. "They say that before the Tree of Peace was planted, nobody's life was safe. Why, our Five Nations even fought among themselves! My grandfather used to tell many stories of those days. One especially, I remember."

"Tell it to me," I begged.

She went over to the water jar, hanging from a roof pole, and dipped a gourd-full, offering a drink to Carrying-Woman, who had just come in, and to me before taking one herself.

"In those days," she began, returning to her seat, "our Onondaga people lived farther north than now. My grandfather, my grandmother and her sister were in their sugar camp, far away from any village, when the attack came. You know how each *oh-wah'-jee-yah,* or big family, owns certain groves of sugar trees, and every spring they gather sap and make sugar."

"Yes," I said, "we do the same thing among the Lenapes." These trees are now called "sugar maples" by the English.

"Grandfather was out hunting the day it happened," she continued, "instead of gathering sap from the trees

with his sled and bark barrel as usual. Grandmother and
her sister were keeping up the fires beneath the big clay
pots where the sap was boiling. It was hot in the cabin
and they stepped outside to get a breath of cool air. Suddenly Grandmother saw a man, a stranger, slip from one
tree to another, hiding behind it."

"She must have been frightened," I put in.

"Truly! The two women rushed back into the cabin
and set the door in place. It was a strong one, made of
heavy elm bark on a pole frame."

"I know that kind," I remarked. "It is made strong
to keep wild animals out while the cabin is not in use."

"They braced the door with a wooden corn pestle
and some sticks," she went on. "They feared the strangers
might have found Grandfather and killed him. All was
silent for a while; then they heard little screech-owl calls
around the cabin. It was a party of raiders; now they
knew it."

"What happened then?"

"Suddenly a stone hatchet crashed through the door.
It chopped and chopped to make a hole big enough for
a man to enter. Soon a warrior started to crawl through
the hole."

"What did the women do? What could they do?"

"They were smart," Among-the-Blossoms said
proudly. "They filled large wooden ladles full of boiling sap. When the first man was almost through, they
dashed the scalding sap in his face. Blinded, he crawled
screaming about the floor. But the women screamed
louder so those outside would not know what had happened. Every man of that raiding party, six in all,

crawled into that cabin. Every man was creeping blinded, upon the floor, when Grandfather came home with his deer. He said they were Flint People—Mohawks."

"*Gweh!*" I exclaimed with a shudder. "Those were brave women. What did your grandfather do?"

"He was going to kill them; but Grandmother said no. She said, after all, they were *On'-gweh On'-weh,* Real People, or Iroquois. So she doctored their burns with sunflower seed oil; and Grandfather bound them and took them all back to *On-on-dah'-geh* town. Our chiefs notified the Mohawks that we were holding six of their warriors. 'We liked them so much,' the message ran, 'That we gave them a sugar feast; but they were greedy and took too much.' Grandfather said the Mohawks paid a high price to get their men back. One of the warriors never got entirely well from his burns. He was blind in one eye until he died."

"I suppose the Five Nations never fight among themselves now," I ventured.

"Only with words around the council fire," said Carrying-Woman, "or with ball and racquet upon the playing field. Some day we hope that all nations will join us beneath the branches of the Great Tree of Peace."

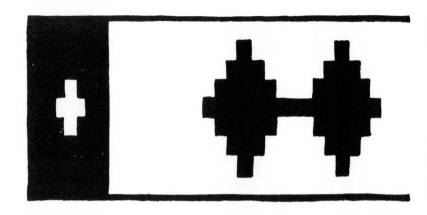

VIII. GATHERING CLOUDS

Our new home under the shed had, among its advantages, the fact that "our women" could cook for us. Of course my companions still had to work for our supplies. Although Many-Tongues' arm was now practically well and he was able to bring in a rabbit now and then, he was no deer hunter. And of course we had no garden. I could not bring myself to let Among-the-Blossoms hunt, although she suggested it; but she and Carrying-Woman helped other women of the village at various tasks, for which they were paid in corn and deer meat. Also they went on occasional berry-picking trips. And of course I was helpless—worse than useless.

I worried more about that after the bruises cleared up and I could move any part of my body freely—except that wretched right lower leg. The slightest movement of that brought agonizing pain, splint or no splint. Moonhakee seemed to feel my misery; he insisted upon getting up on my bed beside me whenever I was left alone.

When the women were embroidering the shoulder pouch, it was not so bad. They sat near on a big rush mat and I could watch every movement. The girl was doing the strap and Mother the pouch itself.

I marvelled to see the tiny stitches they made with nothing but sharp bone awls and fine sinew thread. Under these stitches, which had to be placed exactly right, they worked the colored quills—red, yellow, black and white—to form pretty patterns. I noticed they always flattened the quills with little bone paddles and kept them wet and pliable in a bowl full of water while they were working. Finally the pouch was finished—a beautiful thing—and was delivered to the doctor to pay for setting my leg. He had furnished the materials—deerskin, colored quills, even sinew.

Next day Carrying-Woman appeared with an armful of buckskins and a borrowed cutting board.

"Now we are going to make *ah-tah'-gwah*—moccasins," she announced. "Five pair will go to pay for these skins; the rest we can trade for what we need."

"Listen," I said, "I am tired of being useless. Fix me so I can sit up, and give me that cutting board. I'll make the moccasins, you two make them pretty."

"You don't know how!"

"Just watch me!" I insisted. "In Lenape land I was servant to an old lady for a while—she taught me!"

With one of the pack frames and a few sticks and thongs the women fixed me a sort of backrest so I could sit up in comfort. What a relief!

Now Mother laid the cutting board across my lap, and brought me one buckskin, a little deerskin sack full

of sharp flint flakes, a bone awl, a hank of deer sinew and
a knotted thong that recorded the measurements of a pair
of moccasins someone had ordered.

"Now let's see what you can do!" she challenged.

I examined the cutting board, a fine old one, golden
brown in color, its edges polished from long use; I should
say it was two feet long by fourteen or fifteen inches wide
and an inch and a half thick. Probably it had been split
from a seasoned log with deer horn wedges and ground
smooth with bits of sandstone.

The measuring string had a knot on each end and
one near the middle; the length from the middle knot to
the more distant end was the measurement from toe to
heel; the other, the measurement around the foot at its
widest part.

I called for a bit of charcoal, and with this and the
measurement string I laid out a moccasin on the buckskin as shown in the drawing, cutting it out with the sharp
flint flakes discarding each when it became dull and se-
lecting another. Then using the first moccasin as a pattern I cut out its mate. They were made all in one piece.

"Fine!" said Among-the-Blossoms. "But I don't like
to see you doing women's work."

"Did anyone ever see you shooting with a bow and
arrow?" I asked softly. She did not answer, my point was
won!

I took a shred of sinew, moistened it with spittle,
twisted it on my bare thigh into a cord, thin, but strong;
I tied a knot in one end. Now I punched a hole with the
awl in the very tip of the future moccasin and pulled the
cord through. Then I caught it through each side alter-

nately, as the picture shows, finally pulling it tight and straightening the resulting puckers with the awl's point. That formed the toe; the heel was merely a matter of straight sewing. My first moccasin was made.

In the meantime the two women had been ornamenting with quills the narrow strips of skin to be sewed on over the puckered toe seams; decoration of the flaps came later.

We made moccasins day after day until no more skins could be found; we had plenty of orders, for people liked our product.

We were puzzled as to what we could do next to earn our food. But finally our clever women decided on making pots, although I feared I could not help in this work. It was true I had learned how to make Lenape earthenware, but this appeared to be different. It seemed as if the plan should succeed however, especially as Onondaga pottery is usually better formed and decorated than Seneca.

While my three companions, together with a village girl who had offered to guide them, were away looking for suitable clay, I happened to notice the pile of dulled flint flakes I had discarded during my moccasin making, and an idea struck me.

I called to a little boy who was passing and succeeded in making him understand that I wanted the flakes and a bone awl from a nearby shelf in the shed. When he brought them to me, I started in.

First of all I laid a scrap of deerskin in my left palm, placing one of the flakes on it; this I clamped down firmly with my finger tips. Then taking the bone awl in my right hand I pressed it against the edge of the flint. At once a little scale flew off from the bottom of the flake. I repeated the process, turned the flake this way and that, pressing off chips, until I had a neat little arrowhead with a stem, the same as I used on my own arrows. Going ahead with the work I had about twenty finished when my companions came home. I showed them a handful.

"Where did you get the Bark-Eater arrowheads?" Many-Tongues asked.

"I made them," I said proudly, "made them to trade."

"Nobody would trade for these," said Among-the-Blossoms.

"Why not?" I demanded, offended.

"They are not *On'-gweh On'-weh* style. Our arrowpoints are long and slim and beautiful. We don't like these clumsy stems."

In a flash of anger I threw all the arrowheads outside the shed; but Among-the-Blossoms, with a sigh, went out and picked them up again.

"Better use them on your own arrows," she said patiently as she handed them back to me, "until they are gone, then make our style. You must remember you are *On'-gweh On'-weh* now, not Lenape."

Next day I found the courage to make some more arrowheads; this time long slim triangles without stems —Iroquois style. But it was hard to trade even these; the trouble was, they were easy to make and every man knew the art. Then I thought of making complete arrows; but when I realized I had no seasoned sprouts for material, and no feathers, I gave up that idea. So I lay back and watched the pottery making.

They had brought in the clay in a couple of old worn-out robes; now the three of them pounded it with stones until it was pulverized; then ran it through their fingers to get out pebbles, sticks and trash. Even this was not enough to suit; they sifted it all through two basket sieves —first a coarse one, used ordinarily for hominy; then a fine one. Now they moistened the whole mass and kneaded it like dough.

"Isn't that too much?" I asked. "Most of it will dry out again before you can use it."

"That is just what I want," Carrying-Woman explained. "This is what we shall work with—" she set aside a good-sized chunk, "and these I shall keep for another day." She rapidly shaped the remainder of the clay into loaves and laid them on a piece of bark to dry.

"Should you use this clay just as it is, or mix something with it?" I asked.

"I don't really know," she replied. "I have never used this clay before. But it seems very fine, and I am afraid it will crack unless I mix it. Anyhow mixing will do no harm."

At this, Many-Tongues brought forward a piece of rotten, gritty stone, and a slab and a round cobblestone to grind it with; the resulting grit was run through the two sieves, and finally mixed with the clay; it looked to be about one-fifth of the total bulk.

Now Carrying-Woman made a ball of the wet mixture and sticking her thumbs into one side, quickly shaped a rude vessel which she clapped into a round wooden bowl; and pressed and worked it with her fingers and a piece of gourd until the clay stood up above the wood about an inch all the way around. This was to be the bottom of the new pot. The next step was to roll out a long strip of clay on the wooden cutting board until it was about as thick as my thumb. This she flattened and applied to the inside of the clay rim, pinching off the end where it was too long. Finally she smoothed and blended it with her fingers and the gourd tool.

So she continued, building up the pot, coil by coil, each one above and inside the last. I noticed she always kept her fingers and the gourd smoothing tool wet as she blended the coils and shaped the growing pot.

Her product turned out to be round bodied, with a straight neck, at the top of which she added a coil on the outside, shaping it to make the collar seen on most Iroquois pots.

"What's that for?" I questioned. "Lenape pots don't have collars!"

Many-Tongues did not hesitate to answer.

"Just like a Bark-Eater, to ask such a thing! Anybody can see it makes the pot strong—hard to crack. And if you want to use your pot for a bucket and put a handle on it, the collar will keep your rope from slipping off."

Now Carrying-Woman trimmed and smoothed the whole pot, except the bottom, very carefully and set it aside to harden while she started another. Later in the day, when the pot was dry enough to handle, she took it out of the wooden bowl and finished its bottom; then she polished it all over with a smooth wet pebble. Now came the decoration of the collar, which she did with the point

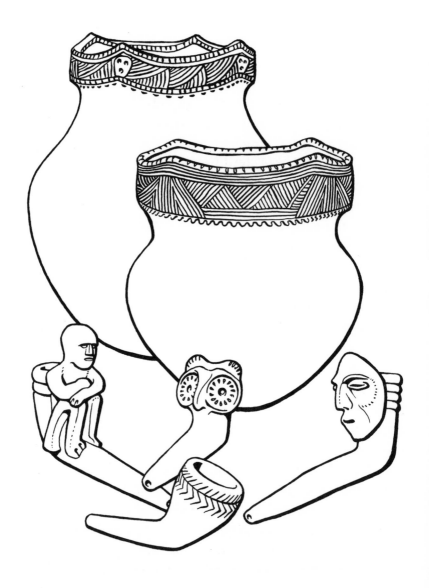

Artifacts of clay: pots and pipes.

of a bone awl, drawing short straight lines at different angles, to form patterns, very evenly and carefully all the way around. At one point the collar had dried too hard and she had to dampen it with a piece of wet buckskin before she could scratch in the pattern.

The pot was a beauty, graceful in shape and pleasing in decoration. Moreover it had a flat round bottom and would stand alone. The pointed bottom Lenape pots I knew how to make seemed poor beside it. In the meantime Among-the-Blossoms had made a similar pot, not quite as perfect, perhaps, but a fine one.

It must have been ten days later, when the first batch of pots was quite dry, that they baked them, building the fire at one side of the shed so I could watch. First of all they set them all around the fire, on their sides, mouth to the blaze, at some distance; then gradually moved them nearer and nearer, as they grew hotter and changed color. When the fire had burned down to coals, they rolled the hot pots with sticks into the middle of it and turned them mouth down; then piled rotten wood over them, covering all. Soon the mass became white hot and glowing, including the pots. Resting then, they let the fire burn down to ashes; then rolled the pots out with sticks. They were perfectly fired and rang clear when tapped. A dull sound would have meant one or more cracks.

Carrying-Woman had broken up a few corncobs in a mortar; now she threw a handful of pounded cobs into each pot while it was still hot and stirred it around with her stick. As the smoke from the burning cobs gushed from the pots, she explained that this process made them more waterproof.

After the first batch I was permitted to help with the pot making. But there was little I could do, outside of the polishing with a wet smooth pebble, which was turned over entirely to me.

Then I suggested we make clay smoking pipes as well as pottery. And in this I became as good as my teacher, because I had made clay pipes in Lenape land. However, Iroquois pipes are much larger and take many different shapes. There is one with a bowl in the form of a morning glory flower; another with the bowl like a little cooking pot, with collar and decoration, all complete. Others have animal heads or whole animals modelled on the bowl, some a twined snake, or human heads or masks. Like the Lenape pipes, however, the hole through the stem is made by running a thick stalk of grass through the clay when soft and leaving it there to be burned out when the pipe is fired.

Between trading our pipes and pottery for food, Many-Tongues' rabbit hunts, and my companions' numerous berry-picking trips, we were able to live. In spite of this I knew I was a burden on the three of them, and this thought hung over me night and day.

One evening Among-the-Blossoms said to me:

"Tomorrow they are holding the Green Corn Dance in the council house. Do you mind if your mother, Many-Tongues and I take part?"

"No! Why should I object?" I responded. "You three work all the time on my account and gain nothing from it."

Just the same I felt unhappy and deserted in spite

of myself when they all started off in the morning, carrying their bowls and spoons, Among-the-Blossoms wearing her best embroidered dress. Even Moonhakee, I could see, looked after them longingly as if he wanted to go too; but finally he jumped up on my bunk and lay close beside me all the morning. The council house was not far away so I could hear speaking, singing and the rhythm of rattle and drum.

They returned shortly after midday, bringing in a bowl a share of the feast for me. It was a sort of soup, or rather stew, made by cooking green corn scraped from the cob with fresh beans and meat. This kind of corn is sometimes called "twice-chewed" because it is taken from the cob with a scraper made of deer's jaw bone.

Among-the-Blossoms made Moonhakee get down from my bunk so she could sit beside me while I ate, and mother seated herself on a mat nearby, with the boy.

"What did you do at the Green Corn Dance?" I asked.

"The main thing," she said, "was to give thanks to the Three Sisters for our gardens, and to do the Great Feather Dance in their honor."

"What Three Sisters?"

"Our Supporters, the Corn, Bean and Squash Spirits," she replied seriously. "Besides we played the Bowl Game for a while—the Spirits enjoy watching that, you know. This evening there will be pleasure dances!"

"The Lenapes have a Corn Dance, too," I told them, "to give thanks to Mother Corn; but the big thanksgiving ceremony is late in the fall. Then they give thanks for everything and sing their dreams."

"That's nothing," said Many-Tongues. "We have our grand dream feast in the middle of winter; then we kill a white dog to carry our prayers to the Master of Life. The societies all turn out then and we have all kinds of dances and games."

"We have other thanksgiving ceremonies, too," Carrying-Woman put in. "There's Thanks to the Maple, which comes early in the spring when the sugar sap begins to run; then the Thanks for First Fruits when the strawberries are ripe; next comes Corn Planting; then this Green Corn Dance, the Harvest Dance and finally the Hunting Dance to give thanks for the deer and all the other animals we use for meat and skins."

"There!" Many-Tongues said. "You see? We *On'-gweh On'-weh* are more thankful than the Bark-Eaters for what we receive!"

He was trying to tease me, to rouse me up, to make me laugh; but somehow it did not work.

Several days later, after the Green Corn Dance was over, my three companions went away to help some Seneca woman with her garden, leaving me with Moonhakee. I felt especially lonely and helpless. For one reason I got thinking of Little-Bear.

It was common knowledge in this village that the Lenape hostages were all living in the valley of *Jon-nes'-see-yoh* not much more than half a day's journey to the west, and Little-Bear must be among them; yet here I was, helpless, unable to reach him.

My thoughts turned then toward Jamestown. I had not thought so much about that little settlement for months. As I lay on a borrowed bearskin robe staring at the cooking fire, the lazy smoke seemed to take the form of water and again I saw the River James moving slowly along low grassy banks, and the houses built by men of my own kind. The picture was so perfect I could see the little diamond-shaped panes of the windows gleaming in the sun. Was my uncle still loitering away his time in the public house, heavy with the odor of stale ale? And my friends, what of them?

What of my good friend Mataoka, called Pocahontas? Had she really taken ship with her husband, Master John Rolfe and their little son as they had planned? Had she sailed from her native shore for that almost fabulous island across the Great Water?

England! I must have spoken the word aloud, for Moonhakee raised his head from my knee and stared at me, then dropped it again with a sigh and went back to sleep.

England! What memories that word awakened! My mother, busy at her spinning; the spokes of her wheel a blur, her small foot endlessly tapping the treadle; my father, bent over, poking the fire with the black tongs. What were they doing now, this very minute, while their son lay ill, stretched on the skin of a wild beast under a bark roof?

What of my father's claim to his older brother's estate in Lincolnshire, where the tame deer grazed on the vast green lawns or moved like shadows beneath the ancient oaks? But surely my friend Mataoka would find them, she would reach them with news of me.

That evening Many-Tongues went out to visit a friend, and Among-the-Blossoms, as was her custom, seated herself on the edge of my bunk, with Carrying-Woman, as usual, nearby.

"Since I have been lying here," I said, "I have been thinking of many things. The sun has gone down now; but soon the moon will show its face; we sleep, and when we wake the sun will rise again on the opposite side. Who started all this? Where did human beings come from? How did it all begin? The Lenape people tell certain stories to explain it, but I should like to know what the *On'-gweh On'-weh* think."

The two women exchanged glances, then Carrying-Woman spoke.

"Don't you know," she said in mild reproof, "that it is bad to tell stories of this kind in warm weather?"

"Oh, I know," I said. "That's because some little snake or bug might hear and report what we say. But this is different; it is something great; something different from common stories. I am sure no harm will come of it."

"Very well," said Carrying-Woman, rather doubtfully, "I'll tell you. We do not know when the first beginning took place . . . I do not think there ever was a beginning. The oldest story we know says there was a tribe of people living up in the sky; where the earth is now was nothing but water."

"About these sky people," I asked. "Were they men and women just like us?"

"No, they were full of magic power; yet they could be mean and jealous, just like humans. If the chief of the sky world had not been jealous of his wife, the earth would never have existed."

"How did that happen?"

"The chief became sick, and he dreamed that a certain tree that grew near his cabin had been pulled up. This was a wonderful tree called 'Tooth' and its flowers gave out light to the sky world. Then someone guessed the chief's dream, and told him that the tree should indeed be uprooted, and that his wife should be thrown into the hole, to satisfy his dream and cure his illness.

"So the chief ordered the tree to be uprooted, and he urged his wife to look down into the hole. When she did so, he pushed her in; then they replanted the tree called 'Tooth.' And all this happened because the chief was jealous of his wife."

"You have not told why he was jealous," I reminded her.

"It was whispered that two different men had been seen talking to his wife. One was Fire-Monster-with-the-White-Body; the other, Northern-Lights."

"What happened to the woman?" I asked.

"She fell down through the hole in the sky, down, down toward the waters which covered the earth. The ducks swimming on the water, saw her coming and flew up to break her fall. On their backs she slowly fell.

"Then the different water animals contended for the privilege of receiving her when she reached the water. Finally the turtle was chosen. Then the otter, the beaver and the muskrat dived down to get earth to place on the turtle's back. Only the muskrat succeeded. The turtle with the earth on his back grew and grew until he became the great island where we live today. This turtle was *Hah-nyah-denh-go'-nah,* the turtle you were named for. Think you can remember that?"

"I'll try. What happened to the Sky-Woman?"

"The ducks let her down softly upon the new island; through the power of the Sky-Chief, her husband, she was given enough to eat. After a while her daughter, Breezes, was born and this one grew rapidly. Some say she married the West Wind; others say that an Under Water Person was the father of her children."

"So the girl had children?"

"Yes, twin sons; one was born in the natural way; the second, impatient, burst through his mother's body and killed her. The first one was Good-Mind, or Sapling, sometimes called the Holder-of-the-Heavens; the second was Bad-Mind, sometimes called Flinty or Warty."

"Is there any more to the story?" I asked.

"Yes, a lot more," Carrying-Woman went on. "Good-Mind not only created men and women, but he went about making all sorts of good and useful things so they would be happy. Bad-Mind created poisonous and evil things, and was always trying to spoil his brother's work. When Good-Mind created deer and all the animals useful to man, it is said that Bad-Mind shut them up in a cave and his brother had to find them and release them. But not all found their way out; those that remained became *ot'gon,* monsters, full of evil . . ."

A sizzling, dazzling flash of lightning cut off her words—a crash of thunder rocked earth and sky. With a scream Among-the-Blossoms clutched my arm. Then came a gust of wind which nearly overthrew our old shed, and a torrent of rain.

"You see," she whispered, "what comes of talking about such things in the summer!" We had been so absorbed in the story we had not noticed the approaching storm. From that time on until frost I could not get either of them to tell any kind of story. In fact I was impressed myself.

The days dragged on; more and more I felt my own uselessness; I was nothing but a burden. Sometimes I wished I might die. And I thought more and more about Tadoda'ho. That he would meekly swallow the message I had sent him through Big-Nose, seemed more and more unlikely. More and more I felt sure that he would try again to injure us, and this time he might succeed even better.

However, although I did not see it then, those days that seemed so empty and hopeless were really beneficial. I learned so much Onondaga that from that time on, I seldom had to ask a meaning, or how to express myself. At the same time I learned a lot of Seneca, which is similar in many ways. Many-Tongues said that so far as interpreting the talk between "our two women" and myself was concerned, he might as well go home.

The moon that was full that night soon grew old and disappeared; another had taken its place, and yet another; the leaves had begun to change color and the nights were chilly when I found I could walk again, slowly and painfully, leaning on my companions, but really walk, which showed that the bone had knit. However, there was a running sore on the same leg that refused to heal, and my spirits were still very low.

"We must do something about that sore," Among-the-Blossoms said one day. "The herb poultices the doctor told us to put on it do no good. And there is something wrong inside you, too; you never laugh or smile any more. Is your heart bad because of me? Because I came on this trip when you did not want me?"

"Don't say such things," I answered. "If I am discouraged, it is partly because I know I am nothing but a burden on Mother's shoulders and yours. Twice, now, you have saved my life. You should have let me die."

It is a good thing Carrying-Woman came in just then and the subject was changed. Among-the-Blossoms called her attention to the sore, however; and she could see herself it was no better.

"Have you ever thought of trying the curing societies?" Mother asked. "These Big Mountain People have two truly good ones—the *Ho-dee-gon-sa-sonh'-onh* or Company of Faces and the *Nay-gah-nay-gah'-ah* or Little Water Society."

"How do they work?" I asked, not much interested.

"The Faces drive away disease when it is caused by evil spirits, or magic power like witchcraft, or something inside the sick person; the Little Waters have a special medicine for wounds and sores."

"Are their fees high? If so, it's no use. You two have nearly worked your fingers off already, trying to pay the doctor who mended my leg."

"They do not charge any fees!" Mother replied. "All you have to do is to provide the kind of food that they like when they meet to doctor you. The Faces like a certain kind of pudding; the Little Waters a boiled bear's head and corn soup."

"I doubt if they could help me," I growled. "Why take all that trouble?"

"Hush!" said Among-the-Blossoms. "Listen to me. We are going to keep on trying until you are cured. Understand?"

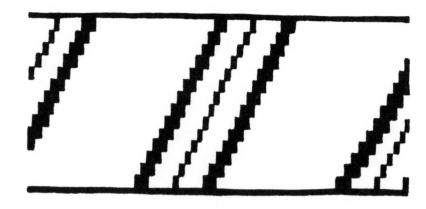

IX. I DEFY TADODA'HO

Finally I gave in to my friends and agreed to let the curing societies work upon me; the one for my festering deep sore; the other to drive away my "bad heart," the cloud of black thoughts which hung over me most of the time. And then we found there were no Little Waters at all and but very few Faces in the village where we were staying; we would have to move on to a larger town.

"Truly it is bad," Among-the-Blossoms lamented, "that we must leave this village before you are really well. We know the people here now, and the three of us can work and earn all the food we need. Moreover, we have a place of our own to live in. Yet, it seems, that you cannot get well if we stay."

The trip west from the village to the great town of *Gah-nun-dah-say'-geh* in the beautiful valley of *Jon-nes'-see-yoh* should not have taken more than half a day; but I had to walk so slowly and rest so often that it was late in the afternoon when we arrived.

No one barred our passage and we made our way to the public square, where we found a crowd of people gathered around the large council house.

"Some great excitement is afoot," I said. "I wonder what it is."

"Better forget the excitement," Carrying-Woman advised. "The first thing for us to do is to find a place to stay so you can lie down and rest."

"I don't think that can be done just now," I argued. "By the looks of it, none of the women are at home."

"I'm going to find out all about it," said Many-Tongues. "You three stay right here so I can locate you when I come back. It will not take me long. From what I just overhead some famous chiefs must be in that council house making speeches." He plunged into the crowd. Soon he came worming his way back. He looked pale and scared.

"I was right, Hiawatha himself is speaking in there. But," he whispered, "a runner has just come in from Onondaga; he has a message for you. I am afraid this means trouble!"

Before he could tell us any more we heard the call of the runner, *"Go'-weh, Go'-weh, Go'-weh!"* and the crowd fell back.

Now we saw him—a thin, hard-faced young man clad only in breechclout and moccasins, and carrying in his hand a short string of white shell beads or *oht-goh'-eh* now known as "wampum."

"Where is Big-Turtle, the adopted Bark-Eater?" he demanded.

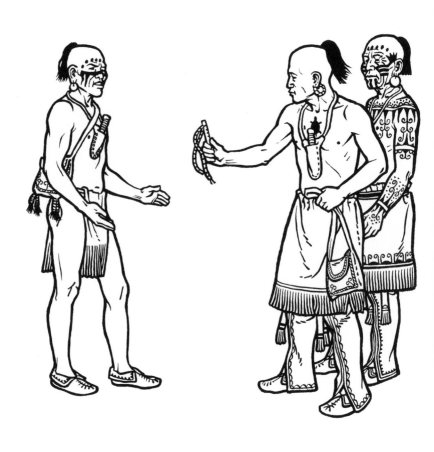

"I am Big-Turtle," I replied in Onondaga. He handed me the beads.

"This string will confirm a message from Tadoda'ho, to Big-Turtle."

"What is it?"

"Tadoda'ho commands you to return to *Gah-nah-dah-go'-nah* at once. He wishes to talk with you."

I noticed out of the corner of my eye that my companions were watching anxiously to see what I would do.

Then I thought of the time we had lost and all we had
suffered on Tadoda'ho's account and my indignation
flared.

"You tell Tadoda'ho for me," I said, "that he has
already planted many thorn bushes in my path; these
have delayed me so much that the errand which brought
us here is not yet finished. If he wishes to talk with me,
let him come here himself!"

The runner blinked.

"Truly do you wish me to carry such a message to the great chief Tadoda'ho who has honored you with wampum? He will be angered. Indeed he is powerful and possesses means to make those suffer who do not obey him."

"Carry the message as I have spoken it!"

"With what shall I confirm it?" the runner asked.

I handed him back the string of shell beads he had given me.

"It is not proper to return the same string!" he protested.

"I have no other," I said. "You and Tadoda'ho must be satisfied with this."

He shook his head, and slipping the string into his shoulder pouch, walked away muttering.

"Those were brave words," said Among-the-Blossoms. "But they may cause your death."

"And ours, too," added Carrying-Woman. "The grand Head Chief of the Five Nations does not send special messengers with wampum for nothing."

"It was not brave at all," I said. "What does he think I am? A leaf blown by the wind? He cannot expect me to give up my search for Little-Bear after we have worked and suffered so much. And all on his account, the old skull-face. What is he to me, that I should obey him? He may try to punish me, but I do not think that even Tadoda'ho would be wicked enough to revenge himself on you three."

However, in my heart I was not so sure, and when my anger had cooled, I almost regretted the stand I had taken.

Of course all this was seen and heard by many people, some of whom, doubtless, understood the Onondaga language. Before I was through discussing what had happened, the crowd parted again to make way for three remarkable persons.

First was a kind-faced elderly man with a high forehead. His long hair, streaked with gray, hung loose, but carefully brushed, about his shoulders. He was not tattooed. Behind him stalked a fat pompous old man with a big mouth and an Iroquois scalp lock like my own; his neck, chest and arms were covered with fine tattooed designs. Behind him a spare, white-haired woman limped along with a staff. On her back she carried a long thin bundle carefully swathed in fine deerskin. I thought it must contain something important, for the ties were wrapped with colored quills and ornamented with deerhair tassels, dyed red.

The leader addressed me in Onondaga, speaking in a low, husky voice.

"Are you the bold young man who just now defied the great chief Tadoda'ho?"

My heart nearly stopped and then seemed to rise up into my throat. Was retribution overtaking me so soon?

"I refused to obey his command; but truly I had a very good reason," I said as bravely as I could.

"I hear Tadoda'ho planted thorn bushes in your path. Will you tell us about them?"

I hesitated. I realized this man must be someone important, and he seemed friendly; yet—

"Would you mind telling me who you are?" I asked.

Instead of answering, he asked me another question.

"Is it true that you are an adopted Onondaga of the Turtle Clan?"

"Yes, truly," I replied.

"Then I am simply a fellow tribesman and fellow clansman of yours. The reason I asked about the thorn bushes was that Tadoda'ho planted some in my path many years ago, and I know how you feel."

At this the fat man broke in with a loud, booming voice.

"Boy, you are talking to the great Hiawatha (*Hah-yah-went'-hah*): I am Deganawi'da (*Day-gah-nah-wee'-dah*)." Pointing to the elderly woman at his side, he continued, "This is Jigon'sasay (*Jee-gon'-sah-say*) the Peace Woman, Mother of Nations, a chief of the Neutral Nation and most wise in council. We three are planters of the Great Tree of Peace, Founders of the Five Nations League. Our names are in everybody's mouth."

"*Skeh-nong'-hah!* Slowly! We are no better than anyone else," Hiawatha chided; and then, addressing me, he continued: "Now, my young friend, tell us about Tadoda'ho's thorn bushes."

When I found who my questioner was, I became so flustered I must have forgotten all my new-learned Onondaga, for I could not think of a word to say. However Many-Tongues was not bashful, and between him and the two women our story was finally told and truthfully, except they gave me too much credit.

Hiawatha seemed pleased and again addressed himself to me.

"Truly then, my son, you have not found Little-Bear yet?"

"No, my father," I replied, glad for the chance to call the great one "father."

He smiled. "I think I can find him for you if you will stay in this town for a few days, or, at least, I shall be able to tell you where he is."

"I thank you, my father!" That was indeed wonderful news.

Then Hiawatha noticed the bandage on my leg, which forced me to go without leggings.

"What is that?" he asked.

"*Hee-yah'-tah-gah-yah'-ee,* nothing at all," I told him—but Among-the-Blossoms set him right.

"It's an old deep sore, and it won't heal. His heart is bad, too—most of the time. We want the Little Waters to doctor him for the sore and the Faces to cure his bad heart, but we have no corn to make the food they require."

"Perhaps I can help you with that also," said Hiawatha. "Anyone who is smart enough to outwit Tadoda'ho and brave enough to defy him is a friend of mine. Not that Tadoda'ho is my enemy now, but he was once, many years ago."

"I am not smart; the smart ones are these friends of mine," I protested. "These two good women and this boy. I am not brave either, although I may be a little reckless when I am angry. But I am proud to have you call me 'friend.' "

Hiawatha called to one of the local chiefs who was in the crowd and asked him to find us bunks in the Turtle Clan long-house and a Turtle woman who would feed us. We followed this man and soon all the arrangements were made and I was lying on a bunk resting.

Before we could plan what to do next, Hiawatha came in, bringing good news.

"You are lucky, my son," he said. "The Little Waters are going to sing for their medicine tomorrow night, and the Song-Holder told me they would doctor you if you will sit with them through the ceremony and give them a little tobacco. Have you any?"

"Unfortunately, no, my father," I replied.

"I thought not," he said. "So I brought some for you." He handed me a packet from his shoulder pouch. "Tobacco" in Onondaga is *oh-yen'-gwah;* in fact that word is about the same in all the Iroquois languages.

"Don't we have to furnish the food?" Carrying-Woman asked.

"No, that is already arranged for. It is a regular meeting of the Society, you see. But you can help the Feast Makers tomorrow if you like; the meeting will be in the large cabin north of this long-house; I think it's the third house."

I stayed in bed most of that day; but those two wonderful women went to the cabin, and when they came back late in afternoon they reported everything was ready for the meeting, including the bear's head and the corn soup.

"Did you boil the head?" I asked Among-the-Blossoms.

"No, we had no kettle big enough. We roasted it."

"How?"

"Well, if you must know, we dug a hole in the ground and built a hot fire in it; then just a little while ago we pulled the burning sticks out and put the head in."

"Was the hair on it?" I asked, to tease her.

"Of course not, silly; it was skinned. All we had to do was to wrap it up in cornhusks and bury it; first with hot coals and ashes; then we filled the hole up to the top with dirt. It will be well cooked when the right time comes tonight."

"How do you make corn soup?" I demanded.

"What do you want to know for? You'll never have to cook any. But I'll tell you. First you boil the corn with ashes until the hulls loosen."

"I should think the ashes would make it taste bad," I remarked, although I knew better.

"Haven't you seen me wash corn after it's been boiled in ashes? What do you think a corn-washing basket is made for? I take it down to the creek and wash it in a basket until the hulls have floated away and boil it again until the taste of ashes is all gone; and that's what we did today. Then we cooked it with meat and beans, and that makes corn soup."

Many-Tongues and I went to the cabin shortly after sunset, only to be stopped at the door by a guard. After we had explained that I was to be doctored he stood aside to let me enter. But he blocked my companion until, after a moment's quick thinking, I told him that I needed my friend to help me in case I had one of my weak spells.

Once inside I saw that there was a low fire burning in a shallow pit in the center of the building, and a small platform or altar had been built at the far end. A man sitting on the left of the fire rose as we entered, led us to the altar and told us to deposit our tobacco. I was about to place mine in a large polished wooden bowl that stood on the altar when he stopped me, guiding my hand to a small cornhusk basket near by. I had slipped Many-Tongues part of my tobacco, so we were both prepared. We turned back and seated ourselves on the edge of a bunk near the door.

Soon men and women began to come in and each went up to the altar, said a few words, deposited some tobacco in the basket, then emptied the contents of a package into the bowl, before finding seats on the edges of the bunks. About twenty came in, I think, and there they all sat in silence, dimly seen in the flickering firelight.

Finally a man rose, and walking over to the fire pit began to throw upon the coals something he took pinch by pinch from a small basket in his hand, muttering as he did so. The man was praying, and as the smoke drifted toward me I recognized the odor of tobacco. At last he finished and threw the basket itself in the fire to be consumed; it blazed and flickered for a moment.

Then the man straightened up and began to speak, in the Big Mountain or Seneca language of which I could understand little. Many-Tongues told me afterward that he was telling the story of the medicine. Away back in the past, it seems, there was a man who was always kind to the animals and birds of the forest. But one day he was shot down from ambush and his scalp taken by an enemy. Then the birds and animals he had befriended gathered, and each contributed something to a medicine which was so powerful that they cured the man with it, and they even recovered his scalp and made it grow back upon his head. This was the *Nay-gah-nay-gah'-ah* or Little Water Medicine, the knowledge of which was passed down from that day until the present by the society founded for that purpose.

The man who had spoken, then picked up a large sack which he had brought in with him and made the rounds of the company, giving to each of us, even to Many-Tongues and myself, a big rattle made of gourd, which he took from the sack. Now a woman came in with a large wooden bowl and a bark ladle making the rounds; each took a drink of the contents, muttering words which meant "I give thanks to our grandfather."

The fire had burned very low, so low we could hardly see, and I had not recognized the woman, but when she reached me I knew those hands, strong yet shapely, that held the bowl. I looked up; sure enough, it was Among-the-Blossoms! I drank a ladle-full of the bowl's contents. It turned out to be a refreshing drink made from berries and water.

After I had dropped the ladle back into the bowl I expected her to go on to the next, but Among-the-Blossoms stood fast. "Aren't you going to say the words?" she whispered. Then and only then I remembered to give thanks to "our grandfather" and she went on, offering the bowl to Many-Tongues, next in turn.

When she had left the cabin, someone pulled ashes over what remained of the fire, and we sat in total darkness, except for a little moonlight coming in through the smoke hole.

Then I noticed a very strange thing; the contents of the bowl on the altar was glowing with a soft ghostly light. "Do you see that light?" Many-Tongues whispered. "It's the medicine!"

Now the people began to shake their rattles, gently at first, then stronger and stronger. It was not a sharp rattle, but a rushing sound, like rain on the forest leaves, but it had a steady beat. I soon learned to make the sound myself by shaking the rattle round and round instead of up and down.

Now they began to sing, a strange song, sweet, yet different from anything I had ever heard—a song that seemed to carry you back into the past, to the beginning of the world. And so they sang—I mean we sang, for I joined in after a while—all night long; indeed until the east was white with the coming dawn. There were two intermissions, if I recall, when the fire was rekindled and the members of the society rested, smoked and chatted; then Among-the-Blossoms brought in another bowl of berry drink, after which the cabin was darkened and the singing began again.

It was, I think, in the second intermission when a man, a stranger to me of course, brought a little bowl full of liquid and signed for me to take the bandage off my leg. He filled his mouth with the liquid and squirted it into the sore, after which I had to drink what remained in the bowl. It had a queer taste and made me so sick at the stomach I could not sing for some time; but after a while this feeling wore off. I later learned that it was some of the famous Little Water Medicine taken from the big wooden bowl on the altar—the stuff that glowed —mixed with water from the river which had to be dipped with a downstream motion.

In each of the three singing periods the songs were different; and I remember that the cries of various animals and birds and a haunting flute-like note could be heard in some of them.

Just before dawn after the last song had been sung and the fire was blazing again, Carrying-Woman appeared with the steaming bear's head on a big bark platter. Each of us was supposed to caw like a crow and take a bite of it without touching it with hands; if the biter succeeded in getting a bit of meat the whole crowd cawed gleefully; if not the platter was passed to the next member in gloomy silence. I managed to pull off quite a long strip of tender meat with my teeth, and the cawing was terrific.

The final act took place when big kettles of corn soup were lugged in and the members set their small clay pots and bark buckets in a circle around them. Then Carrying-Woman dipped a ladle-full into each container, round and round until the pots were empty, and each member of the Little Waters had a fair share of soup to take home. They must have divided the medicine in the big bowl on the altar in some such manner, for I know that each member is entrusted with a portion of it. In this way the whole stock of precious stuff can never be destroyed, as might happen if it were all kept together.*

* At a later period the medicine was not mixed in a bowl but was kept in the individual packages which lay open on the altar.

X. MASKED HEALERS

While the Little Water ceremony was going on, I
was so interested I forgot my discouragement. But when
it was over and I found my sore had not been magically
healed, but, apparently, was just the same as ever, the
black cloud came over me again. What a fool I was. Not
only was I a useless drag on my three poor friends, but
I had endangered the lives of every one of them by my
angry defiance of Tadoda'ho; and now I had put the
two women to all this work and trouble for nothing. When
we returned to the Turtle long-house, there they lay already asleep in their bunks, exhausted after the night's
labors.

I turned to Many-Tongues.

"All I have brought to you and to them," I said,
"is hard work and misfortune. And for what? I am worth-
less the way I am, and not getting any better. The best
thing for me to do is to drop out of sight, try to find my
way back south."

The boy stared at me reproachfully.

"I did not think that of you, Big-Turtle; you cannot mean what you say. You could not do such a thing."

"Why not?" I argued.

"In the first place, you are not yet strong enough. You would die in the wilderness."

"All the better," I growled. "I am no good to anybody."

"What about Little-Bear whom you came so far to aid? He cannot be far away. You would not fail him now, would you?"

"I have no strength left to rescue him, nor wit to talk him out of his captivity."

"You will have. But the greatest reason you must not go is the duty you owe to the two women who saved your life."

"They would be glad to get me off their hands; I am nothing but a burden," I contended.

"If you left now I think it would finish them," he persisted. "Anyhow another great loss would be terribly hard."

"You mean . . . ?"

"I am thinking of the boy who was killed."

"*Haht-deh-gah-yeh'-ee,*" I groaned. "That's enough."

"Are you going away, then?" he asked.

"*Hee-yah'!* No!" I almost shouted it.

Among-the-Blossoms sat up in bed, pushing the hair back from her face.

"What is this you are not going to do?" she asked.

"Oh, nothing," I said, ashamed of myself.

"I heard everything," she said, calmly. "We must get

the Company of Faces to doctor you just as soon as we can."

"All that hard work again for nothing!" I said gloomily. "You all have talked so much about those wretched Faces that I see them in my sleep."

"Not really?" She seemed greatly excited. "You have truly dreamed about the Faces?"

"Truly, I have said it." It was a fact; I had dreamed about the Faces, but had not attached any importance to that.

"That is a sure sign you need them to doctor you. Let's get them for tonight." Among-the-Blossoms was much in earnest.

"No, not tonight," I advised. "If you must go through with it, let us all have a good night's sleep first."

"Very well. We'll eat some breakfast now, and then your mother and I will see Hiawatha about calling a meeting of the Faces for tomorrow night."

After being up all night I had developed a pretty good appetite, but all those mean women would give me for breakfast was just bread.

"For ten days bread made of white corn is all you should eat," Carrying-Woman explained, "and no salt. After that the first thing you eat should be white in color. Maybe we can find you some white beans."

"Why can't I eat what I want?" I demanded. "I am really hungry."

"That is the rule of the Little Water Society," Mother replied. "If you wish their medicine to cure, you must follow their rules. At that you are getting off easy. Most people doctored by the Little Waters have to go through a lot of preparation, hide themselves away for ten days and see nobody except the one that feeds them."

Later in the day we heard a crier going through the village. He announced that Hiawatha requested everyone to donate a little corn to Carrying-Woman, mother of Big-Turtle, in the Turtle Clan long-house, so that a curing meeting might be held on behalf of Big-Turtle. Immediately the women began to come in with gifts of corn and we had to scurry about to borrow an elm-bark barrel to put it in.

The next day our two women made the pudding the Society of Faces demands, which took a lot of work. First the corn had to be parched or toasted in a broken clay kettle over hot coals, then ground to meal, sifted and then boiled in water sweetened with tree sugar. To make a little for a family is not difficult; but when enough has to be prepared to serve a crowd, it is a hard task. I'll give Many-Tongues credit; he helped grind the corn in the big log mortar with a heavy wooden pestle in spite of the jeers of certain small boys. Mother and the girl would not let me do anything.

This time the ceremony was held in the council house, because Hiawatha himself had requested it, although usually, the home of the patient is chosen. Anyhow the seats were full, and among the congregation I saw Hiawatha and his two companions.

I was seated on a mat near one of the fire pits, although I would have prefererd to sit on a peeled log about two feet thick and six feet long, which had been placed about halfway between the two pits in the middle of the building.

Suddenly the buzz of talking stopped as we heard a curious whinnying sound and a harsh rattling outside. The noises grew suddenly stronger then died away; then sounded loudly again all around the council house and once more were hushed.

There was a gasp from the crowd; I looked toward the door. The most hideous face I ever saw was peering in! Quickly it was withdrawn and another, even uglier if possible, looked in at the other door, drew back.

Now we heard a violent rattling around the first door, and presently a tall, broad-faced man appeared. His kilt, leggings and moccasins were beautifully embroidered and he wore two crossed shoulder sashes of white deerskin, gay with colored quills. On his head was a cap of quilled deerskin, to the top of which was attached a bunch of reddish hawk feathers, split and curled; in his hand he bore a staff from the upper end of which three small objects dangled by strings; later I saw two were miniature masks, the third a tiny turtle rattle.

He marched in, erect and stately; after him came crawling on hands and knees, a mob of hobgoblins out of a nightmare, rattling and whinnying. The ugly masks were carved of wood with huge lips, crooked noses, staring eyes, deep wrinkles. They wore ragged, moth-eaten fur robes, tattered leggings and worn out moccasins. This sight I would long remember. It was then that I saw for the first time robes made of the skin of some huge, woolly brown animal that was a stranger to me. Later I learned that they came from the fierce wild cattle, now called "buffalo" that live in the open country to the west.

The crawling goblins passed me as they followed

their leader around the council house. I really was afraid of them, although I knew they were men like myself disguised in masks and ragged skins. Finally they seated themselves on the floor. Their stately leader threw a few pinches of tobacco in the fire, prayed in a low voice for a little while, then began to speak. He used the Big Mountain or Seneca language, but I was able to make out that he was telling the story of the origin of the masks. One part, which I could not catch, must have been funny, for the crowd laughed.

When he finished a man carrying a large rattle made of snapping-turtle shell came forward and seated himself astride the log. Slowly he began to strike on the log with his rattle; then he started to sing; soon he was drumming on the log and singing with all his might. Now the hobgoblins scrambled to their feet and started to dance; each shook a turtle or a bark rattle; the din was tremendous.

At last the dance was ended and the doctoring began. First of all two of the ugliest, with huge pouting lips, took their stand at the doors as guards. Then a group of hobgoblins from that wild band gathered around me. One after another thrust his bare hands into the fire pit near me, took out handfuls of hot coals and ashes and rubbed them between his fingers until they were gone; then picking up a handful of hot ashes, he blew them all over me. There must have been at least thirty Faces, eight or ten of whom worked on me; and by the time they finished I looked and felt more like a moving ash pile than a human being.

Finally they filed out, rattling and whinnying, and I knew they went to the council house kitchen, a separate

building, where our two devoted women were waiting to fill their bark buckets with False-Face pudding.

In the meantime, Many-Tongues helped me get the ashes out of my ears and my scalp lock; then, as we waited for the women to finish, I took this chance to ask him about the origin of the masks, explaining that I could not understand the story, as the leader had told it in Big Mountain dialect.

"You have heard the story of the making of the

world, haven't you?" he asked. "You know, about Sky-Woman and her two grandsons, Sapling, the Good-Mind and Flint, the Bad-Mind?"

"Yes," I said. "That is a tale Carrying-Woman related to me while I lay sick."

"Good," he began. "It is said that at one time the Good-Mind was traveling about the earth, creating many things that would be useful to men, when he met a queer hunchbacked person with a very ugly face.

" 'Who are you?' he asked.

" 'I am Hah-doo'-wee,' the ugly one said. 'I am full of evil magic. I am Master of this great island which is the world.'

" 'Strange!' the Good-Mind replied. 'Customarily it is said that I, myself, am Master of the world. If you indeed are the Master, call that mountain and make it come to you.'

"Hah-doo'-wee, it is said, called to the mountain, but it did not come; then Good-Mind in turn called it.

" 'Where is the mountain?' Hah-doo'-wee asked. 'I do not see it. It did not obey your call any better than it did mine!'

" 'Look behind you!' said Good-Mind.

"Hah-doo'-wee looked, but the mountain had moved up so close behind him that he banged his nose against a rock cliff, and the nose has been crooked ever since! Then he admitted that Good-Mind was indeed Master and promised that he, Hah-doo'-wee, would help human beings.

" 'If they will wear masks to represent my face, and dance the way I do, I shall be with them in spirit and will help them drive away sickness,' he said."

Mother and the girl came along while I was still chuckling over the way Hah-doo'-wee banged his nose against the cliff. I had wondered why some of the masks were carved with crooked noses.

"Do you know what you are doing?" Carrying-Woman said. "You are laughing! The Faces have cured you!"

Talking with Many-Tongues after we reached home,

I learned that a mask, to have full power, must be carved on a living tree with chisels made of beaver tooth and then split off with deer-horn wedges. "The Big Mountain people," he said, "do not call the original Mask Being Hah-doo'-wee, which is Onondaga, but Shah-go-jo-weh'-go-wah; they say he lives on 'the edge of the world' and when he walks 'the earth shakes.' He gets his power from a great pine tree, growing in the 'middle of the world' upon which he rubs his turtle-shell rattle. There are many lesser Mask Beings, too.

"Every Spring and Fall," Many-Tongues went on, "The Faces go around to all the long-houses and cabins, dancing and rattling in each to drive away bad spirits and everything evil. It is said they even chase out the mice and the bedbugs! I'd run from them myself; I'm afraid of the Faces. People pay them with pudding and tobacco for dancing in their houses."

"Do they perform in the council house, too, at that time?" I asked.

"Truly! But they put on their biggest dance at our great Dream Feast in the middle of the winter. Then some of the Faces go around and beg tobacco from the people on the benches. Those who refuse them have an unhappy time."

"How is that?"

"The Faces drag them to the fireplaces and throw ashes all over their best clothes," he replied.

"Isn't that something like the curing ceremony?"

"Truly!" the boy chuckled. "It's to cure them of being stingy with their tobacco!"

Next morning we discovered something else. When

Among-the-Blossoms took the bandage off my deep sore
to wash it out with the herb medicine, we saw that very
little matter had formed; indeed from that day it began
to dry up and soon was well—even though we forgot
about my eating "white" food for ten days!

That same morning Hiawatha brought us the wonderful news that he had found out exactly where Little-
Bear was held captive.

XI. THE LOST IS FOUND

"Your brother, Little-Bear," Hiawatha said, "is living in a village called *Go-dah-eh-gehs'-geh,* or Smelly-Mud, about half a day's journey down this river. My companions and I am going there tomorrow, and if you four, and your dog, wish to travel with us, I am sure there would be no objection."

I was delighted. Little-Bear would be found, after all our labor and danger! At last! And I liked the thought of traveling with the three Founders; also Many-Tongues seemed equally happy. But, alas, our two dear women had nothing to say.

It was plain that they were much disturbed about something, and this cast a shadow over my joy. Perhaps, I thought, they feared the vengeance of Tadoda'ho might overtake us even yet, before my errand could be accomplished. I noticed Mother was carrying her axe again, ready for action.

Nevertheless they had everything packed and ready

to travel shortly after daylight. The party did not really get under way for some time, however, for the simple reason that Deganawi'da had overslept.

"It's a wonder you got up at all," Jigon'sasay scolded when he finally appeared. "You're as lazy as a big fat corn worm!"

Deganawi'da grinned. "I had good reason," he boomed, "for not wishing to get up."

"What was that?" the old lady asked, unsuspecting.

"I was dreaming about you!"

"You're an old liar!" she accused, giggling in spite of herself.

"What's the use of getting up early?" he yawned. "We have to travel so slowly, anyhow. The Mother of Nations is not a fast traveler."

"I can walk as fast as you, grandpa," she snapped, "or almost . . ."

"*Hau, oh-neh'!*" Hiawatha broke in. "Come now, let's get started!"

He led the way; I came next in order; and then Many-Tongues, then Hiawatha's bodyguard, followed by Jigon'sasay. Next came Carrying-Woman, Among-the-Blossoms and three other women, wives of the guards, acting as carriers; finally Deganawi'da and the two other guards, bringing up the rear. Moonhakee ran hither and yon as was his custom.

When the sun was half way up the sky, Hiawatha called a halt for rest in the cool shade of a huge elm tree on the river's bank. Jigon'sasay and Deganawi'da, finding a log for a seat, resumed their teasing and joking.

The younger women slipped off their burden frames and went down to the water's edge; the guards stretched themselves on the grass, leaving Many-Tongues and me to sit along with Hiawatha on a mossy mound.

Finally I mustered up courage to ask him a personal question.

"Tell me, my father," I said, "how did you happen to think of founding the great League?"

"People say that Deganawi'da thought of it first," he replied. "And it is true that when I carried the plan to the Flint People (now called Mohawks) they accepted it more readily because Deganawi'da had already come down from the North with a scheme very much like mine."

"But how did you first get the idea, my father?"

"Oh, my son," he murmured as his eyes grew misty, "that was many winters ago."

"How many?"

"About forty-five winters ago the League was founded, but by then I had been working on it several years." I did some quick figuring; the League must have had its beginning about the year 1571.

"The idea first came to me after the death of my best boyhood friend," he continued, "a youth who was very dear to me. We had been hunting in the forest when we discovered the approach of a party of strangers. From their dress, their arms and actions, sneaking separately through the forest, they must have been members of a raiding party. We ran for the village to give the alarm, and I reached it safely; but my friend—did not. His body was found later with an arrow sticking in his back. The raiders were of our own blood—Canoe Portage People (Cayugas).

"From that time on I began to think of the Great Peace. The Cayugas are our brothers; why should they fight us, or we them? When we fight all the time among ourselves, how can we expect to resist outsiders who attack us? Such were my thoughts for years. Then the plan took form—the *On'-gweh On'-weh* tribes must agree to fight no more among themselves; but to join hands against any invader. Each nation should take care of its own affairs as before, I thought; but on matters concerning all five there must be a grand council fire with delegates from each."

"What happened then? Tell me." I begged.

"I began to dream," Hiawatha sighed. "I saw a great tree growing from four white roots which ran east, south, west and north. It was nourished with Peace, Right Living and Power. The Tree grew and grew; its branches spread and spread until not only the *On'-gweh On'-weh* Five Nations, but all nations, even Bark-Eaters" (he glanced at me with a faint smile) "might take shelter beneath it."

"Your Tree is growing very well," I said, "and the Five Nations are sitting beneath it already."

"Truly," he continued, "but it was hard to start and it was watered with blood. I told Tadoda'ho, who was our Head Chief at that time about my plan and he laughed at me; I tried him again a few days later, and he became very angry. 'Do you think I am a fool?' he said, 'I am a great chief here and people obey me. What

would I be if your Five Nations joined hands? Just one
little chief among five. I forbid you to continue with
your silly plan.' "

"But you persisted just the same?" I asked.

"Yes, truly," Hiawatha resumed. "Something in my
heart told me not to give it up. But I began to suffer ill
fortune. My brother was murdered, shot from ambush,
by whom we never knew. My wife and two of my children died, one after the other. Everything I tried to do
ended in failure."

"Was Big Nose helping Tadoda'ho then?" I ventured to ask.

"No, Big Nose was not yet born. I suspected that
Tadoda'ho had planted these thorn bushes, but I could
not prove it. One day he sent for me. When I entered his
house, I saw that he was wearing his snakes, his face was
painted to look like a skull. And his fingers, they never
stopped writhing and twisting like the snakes on his head.

" 'I hear you have been having bad luck,' he sneered.
'That foolish plan of yours may have something to do
with it. Your luck might improve if you stopped talking
about that plan. If you don't, even worse fortune may befall you.'

"Shortly after this, the people of my village put on
a lacrosse game for my benefit, thinking to take my mind
from my troubles. *Ah-geh'!* During the game my last remaining daughter, little more than a baby, followed a
pretty bird out into the ball field; the racing players fail-
ing to see her, knocked her down; she was hurt so badly
that she died.

"It was then that I left the village and camped

around in different places, trying to find some spot where I could mourn for my dead, fast and pray, think and plan, in peace. But everywhere I went the ugly vision of Tadoda'ho with his writhing snakes and twisting fingers would rise up before me and I would have to move on. Finally something told me to leave the Onondaga country altogether and travel east to the land of the Flint People (Mohawks). There I found Deganawi'da, who had the same dream, and you know the rest."

"Yes," piped up Many-Tongues, "and our Grandmother here, Jigon'sasay, showed you how to comb the snakes out of Tadoda'ho's hair!"

"Truly," Hiawatha agreed with a smile, "and she helped us in many other ways. Indeed, she is justly called the Mother of Nations."

"I'll comb the snakes out of Deganawi'da's scalp lock, too," said Jigon'sasay, "if he keeps on teasing me. We women are good at combing out snakes and breaking off horns."

"Come, children," said Hiawatha, "haven't you stopped quarrelling yet?"

"We have been quarrelling whenever we met for nearly fifty years," Deganawi'da grunted, "and it's too late to stop now."

"*Hau, oh-neh',*" urged Hiawatha, "if we do not stop quarreling and start walking it will be night before we reach Smelly-Mud."

Smelly-Mud village stood on a low rise of ground in the valley of *Jon-nes'-see-yoh* on a side stream a few hundred paces back from the main river; at a somewhat greater distance behind it loomed the bluffs that rimmed the valley on the east, with cornfields in between from which all trees had been felled.

"In a few moments," I thought, when we sighted the bark roofs, "I'll be talking with Little-Bear!"

But I reckoned without the ceremonies thought necessary when the great ones visit a humble village. Hiawatha halted us a few hundred paces from our goal; then one of the women bearers brought forward two slim forked sticks and sticking them in the ground laid a shorter straight piece across them; on this Hiawatha hung a string of wampum. Another woman then produced a little clay pot full of ashes, from which she extracted some hot coals. Blowing upon these and feeding them with grass, she soon had a fire started; the smoke rose in a thin column.

After a while a young man emerged from the village, and recognizing Hiawatha, talked with him a while in Seneca. As he turned to go I noticed that he picked up the wampum.

While we were waiting his return, Many-Tongues addressed our leader.

"Is the tale true which people tell," he asked, "that you were camping one time by a small pond on which there were a flock of ducks, and when they flew away they took all the water with them? They say you found some shells in the dry bottom of the pond out of which you made the first wampum."

Hiawatha laughed.

"People make a big story out of a little thing," he said, "I remember the pond and the ducks, but they did not carry the water away when they flew. They made so

much noise, however, that I went over to see what was
going on and I found the tiny shells along the shore. I
punched holes in them to make beads; before that we had
used mostly beads made of bone, or the quills of a certain bird, or even wood, to confirm messages. Later on
we got the regular solid shell *oht-goh'-eh* beads, traded
in from the south."

Now we saw the youth approaching again; he spoke
to Hiawatha and handed him another string of beads.
That confirmed our invitation; but still Hiawatha delayed. "I shall smoke my pipe first," he told the messenger—and proceeded to do so. I fretted inwardly, although Many-Tongues whispered in my ear that it was
bad manners to show too much haste in accepting an invitation. It seemed a long time before we were sitting in
the Smelly-Mud council house, enjoying delicious *oh-
no'-kwa* with boiled corn bread. While we were eating,
I looked about for Little-Bear. Although most of the seats
were occupied, I did not see him.

When we had finished, a fine looking man, whom I
took to be a chief, stood up and made a speech of welcome, I thought, although I could understand but little.
He was answered in turn, and at length, by Hiawatha,
Deganawi'da and Jigon'sasay. During all this I became
very restless; finally I whispered to Many-Tongues that
I was going out to look for Little-Bear; the boy was hor-
rified and urged me to be patient; even Carrying-Woman,
across the building on the women's side, caught my eye
and signalled me to stay where I was. After ages it
seemed, the meeting was over, and I found myself walk-

ing through the village with my companions, guided by one of the local chiefs and Hiawatha himself.

Finally we halted in front of a small bark cabin standing alone; the local chief called out something, I held my breath.

The next minute a broad-shouldered young Seneca emerged from the building, followed by Little-Bear himself. He looked older, thinner, sadder. He greeted the local chief and Hiawatha in Seneca, then he stared at me. Suddenly his eyes seemed to bulge, he dashed forward—"My younger brother!" he whispered in Lenape —we enjoyed a warm brotherly embrace. "My family," he quavered, "do you know anything about them? I have been worrying about them night and day. They must be starving! With Father dead and me here, there is no one to give them meat!"

"I was with them about five moons ago," I said. "They are not starving, for the garden is doing well. While I was there I killed deer for them, and Mother dried a lot of meat. But they miss you and need you; that is why I am here, to find you and try to get you free to go home to them."

"That is a wonderful thing for you to do," he said. "But—how did you get here and who are these?"

"How I reached this place, my elder brother, is a long story," I said in Lenape. "This is my little friend Many-Tongues, who speaks our language; and this—I took Among-the-Blossoms by the arm, "is . . ." I went suddenly tongue-tied, could not say a word.

"She saved your brother's life," put in Many-

Tongues. "And this good woman helped her; then we three helped him to find you."

"That is wonderful," said Little-Bear. "And I thank you all from my heart." Many-Tongues interpreted.

Among-the-Blossoms cast her eyes down. "I think we had all better go away," she said faintly, "and give the two brothers a chance to talk together."

When they had gone, Little-Bear and I went into the cabin, and the young man followed.

"Who's this?" I inquired.

"He's supposed to be my guard, to keep me from escaping. There are four who take turns looking after me; but about all they do is to see I get enough to eat. We go hunting and fishing together, play games, tell stories. Oh, I have learned to talk Seneca—had to learn it. But tell me, how did you come by these clothes, and this Men-gwee scalp lock?"

"It's hard to believe," I answered. "But I'm a Long-House Builder now. I was captured, and they were about to kill me, but those two women persuaded them to adopt me instead."

"How did that ever come about?"

"I'll tell you some time; just now I would rather talk about your own family." The truth was I hated to confess to him that I had a new Indian mother now, after the loving kindness his mother had shown me in Lenape land.

"You said they are not starving. Are they in good health? How is my wife?"

"White-Deer does not look very happy, but she seems

to be well. The baby is happy, though. He doesn't know the difference."

"The baby? What baby?"

"Your son, of course; yours and White-Deer's," I explained.

"*Hoh, shee'-kee!* That's fine! What's his name?"

"They call him *Wah-pay-wee'-pit*—White-Tooth, but I don't know whether that's his real name," I said.

"How about my little brother and my mother? Are they well?"

"As well as could be expected," I answered. Then I told him something of my own movements, because the last time he had seen me I was boarding the ship that was to take me to Jamestown. But I did not tell him all that happened among the Onondagas. Then an idea struck me—maybe Hiawatha could help. I took my leave.

I found Hiawatha outside the council house, kneeling beside Moonhakee, who was whining with pain.

"Your dog has had a bad argument with a porcupine," the great one explained. "Truly his nose is full of quills and I am trying to pull them out for him."

"You should not bother with such a little thing," I protested. "Let me attend to it!"

"I'll finish the work," Hiawatha chuckled. "After all the dog came to me for help, not to you!"

When the quills were all pulled, he informed me that he had found lodgings for us in a private cabin, and that my companions were already there.

"I should like to talk with you a little while, before I join them," I said. He led the way into the council house and we sat down on a bench.

"You know," I began, "that I have come a long way
through many thickets of thorn bushes to find my brother
Little-Bear. Just now, thanks to you, I have talked with
him. He asked me about his family, but I did not dare
tell him everything."

"What didn't you tell him?"

"That his family are really suffering for food, for
there is nobody to hunt for them. Father is dead; little
brother too young; Little-Bear's son is a baby still on the
cradleboard. Then there are our mother, his wife, four
people who are living without meat unless somebody
makes them a gift."

"Why did you not stay and hunt deer for them?"

"I did for a while; but something seemed to tell me
to seek out Little-Bear and try to release him. He, not I,
is the husband and father."

"Now I see it," chuckled Hiawatha, "you wish me
to help you free Little-Bear. How about another hostage
to take Little-Bear's place?"

"I would gladly take his place," I said. "It makes
little difference to me where I live."

"What about your girl friend and your new Iroquois
mother?"

This gave me a jolt. In thinking of Little-Bear I had
actually forgotten them for the moment. Yet I had to say
something.

"They might agree to my staying here," I ventured,
"especially if the great Hiawatha asked them!" In my
heart I doubted it, however.

Hiawatha thought for a few minutes. "I am afraid
it cannot be done," he said at last. "But we might try. I

shall have a council called tomorrow evening to consider the matter."

Rejoining my companions, I found Among-the-Blossoms very silent and thoughtful; she looked up at me two or three times as I was telling about my talk with Little-Bear; but she made no comments, nor did Carrying-Woman. Maybe they expected any moment to see Tadoda'ho's warriors come bursting in. Truly the time was about right for the runner to reach Onondaga and a swift traveling party to return to punish me—cheerful thought! I noticed that Mother was sharpening the stone blade of her axe!

The next day dragged; we were all so excited and worried that we could not settle down to anything; even the dog Moonhakee could not seem to find a comfortable place to lie. Carrying-Woman fussed around a while but finally went out, to "go visiting" she said. Among-the-Blossoms continued in her silent mood and would not tell me what was wrong; several times I caught her looking at me with tears in her eyes. After midday Little-Bear, without his guard, came over to see us, and we talked a little about old times in Lenape land. I noticed that he studied Among-the-Blossoms with great interest, and she him.

I did not reveal to him at first that a council was to be called that evening to decide whether or not he should be released; but when I did tell him, he insisted on going right back to his cabin to pack up his belongings—although I warned him that the outcome of the council was very doubtful.

After Little-Bear had gone I began to think of the

power of the great League that had carried him away
as a hostage, had fed him all this year or more, had provided men to guard him and care for him. And then questions grew in my mind: what made this League so powerful? How did it work? Where did it get its authority?
Tadoda'ho might be Fire-Keeper or head chief, but he
was no king; for I had seen myself that he could not always enforce his will; moreover I knew that even he
would "lose his horns"—be deposed as chief, if he trans-
gressed too far.

So I said to Among-the-Blossoms and Many-
Tongues: "I wish one of you would tell me more about
this Five Nations League and how it works."

Among-the-Blossoms was mending a pair of my moccasins; she glanced up at me, then back at her work without answering. Many-Tongues was chewing on a piece
of dried venison, but he pulled it out of his mouth long
enough to reply.

"I don't feel like talking, either. Anyhow, why do
you ask us when the three people who invented the League
are here? They can speak Onondaga." He stuck the meat
back in his mouth again.

Thus rebuffed I left the cabin, and strolled over to
the council house, thinking not to bother Hiawatha this
time but to try Deganawi'da for a change. A young man
was standing in the doorway, and I questioned him.

"Where is Deganawi'da?"

He grinned and answered me in Seneca—something
I could not catch. When he saw I did not understand,
he made a pillow of his clasped hands, laying his cheek

against it, at the same time snoring loudly, from which I gathered that Deganawi'da was asleep.

Entering the building I saw Hiawatha standing in the middle of a group of men, conversing earnestly; on the opposite side Jigon'sasay sat on a bench with a bevy of women around her. In a far corner, some plump person lay on a mat, covered up, head and all, with a very fancy skin robe. In lulls of the talk I could hear snores.

I sat down on a bench and waited. After a while the men drifted away; Hiawatha noticed me and stepping over to where I sat, dropped down by my side with a sigh.

"*Ah-kee'!*" he said, "I fear I'm getting old. When I stand for so long, it tires me. Did you wish to talk with me?"

"Truly," I said. "Again, my father, I have come to pester you."

"What is it this time?"

"I wish to learn more about the League," I proceeded. "Who would know more about it than you, one of the Founders?"

"You always speak so sweetly," he grinned. "Did you perhaps have maple sugar in your mush this morning? I shall try to answer. But the Tree of Peace has now grown so large I cannot see all of its branches."

"I know that five nations are in the League," I said, "and that the council fire is in the middle of the Long-House which must be in Onondaga country. Is the council fire in *Gah-nah-dah-go'-nah* where I was adopted?"

"There is talk of moving it there," he replied. "But

now it is in an older town about half a day's journey northeast."

"I knew that each nation sends chiefs to the council fire," I went on, "but I have no idea how many delegates there are."

"We now have fifty-one delegate chiefs," he said, "but when Deganawi'da dies, his place will not be filled, as he was the original Founder; he thought of the League first, so there will be only fifty thereafter. When the rest of us die, new chiefs will take up our names and carry on our work."

"How are the delegate chiefs chosen?" I continued.

"In each nation the chieftainships are the property of certain noble *oh-wah'-jee-yah* or families of certain clans. When a chief dies, the head matron of his family simply picks out another one of her men to take up the name of the dead. Then if there is no objection, the new chief is installed by the Grand Council."

"I suppose there are ten delegate chiefs for each of the Five Nations?" I guessed.

"No," he replied. "Some nations have more, some less. The Senecas, our largest nation, have only eight delegate chiefs; the Onondagas, fourteen."

"Why is that?"

"There are only certain noble families who own titles of chieftainship."

"It's all very confusing," I grumbled. "How often do the delegates meet around the council fire at Onondaga?"

"Regularly, once a year," Hiawatha answered. "Then they sing the roll call of chiefs; recite the Great Law;

if any delegates have died, they console the mourners and raise up the new candidates the women have selected to take the places of the dead. Then they decide such matters as need attention."

"Does each delegate have a vote in the council?"

"No, the Senecas and Mohawks on one hand and the Oneidas and Cayugas on the other argue the matter and each group comes to a decision; if the two groups agree, the Onondagas proclaim the result as a decision of the council; if not, the Onondagas try to harmonize the two parties; if this fails the matter is settled by the Onondagas casting the decisive vote."

I pondered on this a while. It sounded like a wise plan. Then I turned to Hiawatha, "Now another thing," I said, "I hear people talking about a chief's horns. You are a chief, but I do not see any horns sprouting from your skull. What about it?"

Hiawatha laughed. "In the early days of the League," he explained, "when a man was installed as chief we set upon his head a cap adorned with deer horns as a badge of office. But fifty-one pairs of horns made the Grand Council look like a herd of bucks; besides, the horned caps were heavy and awkward. So finally we gave each chief a double string of *oht-goh'-eh* or wampum when he was installed and called these 'horns'."

"Now I understand better," I said, "but what happens when a chief 'loses his horns'?"

"That is easy to explain," Hiawatha replied. "If a chief fails to respect his obligations, the leading matron of his family goes to him herself, or sends a messenger with *oht-goh'-eh,* requesting the chief to 'step back into the path.'

"Should he still persist in wrongdoing the matron goes next time with a man of their family and repeats her request.

"And if the chief still does not comply the third time, the matron takes a war chief with her, who simply asks the culprit whether he proposes to reform or not.

"If the answer is 'no,' the war chief takes the 'horns' and gives them to the matron, after which the chief is a chief no longer; he has lost even his name.

"Then it is the duty of the matron to select some other candidate from her *oh-wah'-jee-yah* to 'wear the horns' and carry the name of the chief."

"There is still one more thing," I said. "I have heard that the League not only is inviting the other nations to sit with them beneath the Great Tree of Peace, it is forcing them to do so. Is this true, my father?"

Hiawatha sighed. "Yes, my son, that is true. Tadoda'ho and Deganawi'da are responsible for that addition to the original Plan. I do not know whether it is a good idea or not. Maybe it is. I told you the Tree has now grown so large I cannot see all of its branches.

"We invite the nations to sit with us beneath the Tree. That means that they may still handle their own affairs, but, in return for our protection, they must not make war."

"What if a nation refuses?" I asked.

"Our War Chief, representing the League, holds in one hand white beads of *oht-goh'-eh,* in the other a war club. He makes one last appeal for the nation to accept our plan. If the appeal is refused, he lets the white beads, emblem of Peace, slip through his fingers. Then he uses the war club!"

"I thank you, my father," I said, "I am glad to know these things. But it is plain to me that I can never learn all about the League on one day, or two. Perhaps when we both return to Onondaga land you will instruct me again."

"My son," he replied, "I was born of the Onondagas, but I have not lived among them for many years, not since my trouble with Tadoda'ho, when I lost my dear ones. I joined the Flint people; in fact I carry a Mohawk chieftainship. I am growing old; when this journey with Jigon'sasay and Deganawi'da is done, I think I shall spend the rest of my days in the Mohawk Valley."

XII. THE GREAT CHIEF'S REVENGE

I shall never forget that little council house at Smelly-Mud Village; it was not half the size of that at *Gah-nun-dah-say'-geh,* or the one at *Gah-nah-dah-go'-nah* the scene of my adoption; it boasted only one row of encircling benches.

But that October night it sheltered three of the world's great ones, no less than Hiawatha, and his companions, founders with him of the Iroquois League, who had met with the local chiefs to decide upon Little-Bear's fate. Little-Bear, Many-Tongues and I had been invited to sit with these chiefs at one end of the building; Mother and the girl were seated nearby on the women's side.

Deganawi'da was speaking: his great voice made the bark walls shake. "You all know," he boomed, "why we took hostages from the Lenapes. In following our plan to gather all nations under the Great Tree of Peace, we sent a delegation last year to offer them a very honorable position in connection with our League. As our women are the peacemakers among us, so the Lenape tribes—there are three, you know—would serve as peacemakers for the League.

"Some objected to 'putting on the skirt' as they called it; however, it was finally agreed. But because objection had been offered, and to see that the Lenapes would not forget their promise, we took hostages; Little-Bear is one of these.

"I think it would not be wise to release Little-Bear at this time, because, . . ." he stopped short; a sudden hush fell upon the assembled crowd.

Tadoda'ho, followed by four fully armed warriors had entered the building—was striding toward us, swinging a great war club!

"Now," I thought, "this is really the end of me."

"Where is that little Bark-Eater," he snarled, "who has dared to defy the great Tadoda'ho?" Nobody moved or spoke. "Where is Big-Turtle, I say?"

I turned cold inside, but I forced myself to stand up and step forward. Tadoda'ho recognized me, and fixing me with his glittering eyes, he gripped his club and advanced upon me slowly as I stood there with empty hands.

Suddenly there was a piercing scream; Among-the-Blossoms rushed to me, threw her arms about my neck, tried to shield my body with her own. Gently I disengaged her arms, pushed her off to one side. "This is for me," I whispered. Now I saw Mother charging to my rescue, axe upraised; here came the boy with some kind of weapon. I tried to motion them back.

Now Tadoda'ho was upon me. I saw the club raised
for the fatal stroke. I bowed my head, shut my eyes.

I waited and waited, but no blow fell. "He is playing with me before he strikes," I thought. Then I became
aware that someone was poking me in the ribs. I opened
my eyes. Tadoda'ho was jabbing me with the handle of
his war club.

I looked up at his face. The yellow stumps of teeth
were bared in an almost friendly grin.

"Not bad," he chuckled, "for a Bark-Eater. Now go back to your seat. I shall talk with you privately later."

Shakily, I looked to see what had happened to Mother. Two of his warriors, who had apparently been sitting on her, were now helping her to her feet; one returned her axe. Another released the boy, whose weapon, I now saw was only a stick of firewood.

"I have been testing this young man," Tadoda'ho said, addressing the crowd. "He has done very well and I think

I can use him. What is the purpose of this council?"

It was Hiawatha himself who answered. "Big-Turtle has come here, through many thorn bushes, to seek his brother, the Lenape hostage Little-Bear. Having found him, he asks for his release, offering to take his place. Jigon'sasay and I approve, but Deganawi'da and the local chiefs disagree."

"You could not use Big-Turtle as a hostage anyhow," said Tadoda'ho.

"Why not?"

"He is no longer a Lenape, but an Onondaga by adoption."

"Then you are against releasing Little-Bear?" Hiawatha asked.

"I did not say so. How many Lenape hostages are there?"

"Maybe fourteen or fifteen," said one of the local chiefs.

"Then one more or less will make no difference. I say release Little-Bear." The chiefs looked at him in amazement. But one after another they rose and consented.

Hiawatha turned to Little-Bear. "You are free!" he said in his low, husky voice, using, by force of habit, the Onondaga language.

Little-Bear looked puzzled; I could see he did not quite understand. So standing again, I translated Hiawatha's words into Lenape. I was always proud thereafter that this occasion was my first service as interpreter.

A light seemed to spread itself over Little-Bear's face. I could see he wanted to speak but his feelings were too strong. Finally he murmured, *"Wah-nee'-shih,"* in Lenape.

I turned to Hiawatha. "He says *'Nee-yah-weh'-ha'* —I give thanks," I translated.

"Now there is one thing more," Hiawatha said. "To be sure that Little-Bear reaches home safely, I think we should send two of our warriors with him. Two of the men who were guarding him would be best—they are friends of his. Is it agreed?" After some discussion the chiefs agreed.

I felt a hand on my shoulder. It was Tadoda'ho's. Now he grasped my arm. "You come with me," he said. "I wish to talk with you. And you cannot refuse me this time." My mind was a turmoil as he led me from the council house. I did not know whether to trust him or not.

Once outside he took me out into the bare public square, almost as bright as day in the moonlight, and looked about him.

"No place here for a listener to hide himself. What I wanted to say is this. You pretend to be a Lenape, but you are not. You are one of those strange people from across the Big Water; you call yourselves *Yen'-gees* or something like that. Isn't this true?"

"You are right. I am English—as you call it *'Yen'-gees'*—by birth. But I did not falsely pretend to be a Lenape; I really was one by adoption, before you Onondagas adopted me. How did you know?"

"I have had scouts along the shores of the Big Water just to watch the *Yen'-gees* and inquire into their doings. When they came back and told me that many of that tribe had light skin and sky-color eyes, I knew you must be one of them.

"Now tell me, is it true that the *Yen'-gees* people have strange weapons—magic sticks? All you have to do is to point one at your enemy, then clouds, thunder and lightning come out of the stick and he falls dead?"

"That is not far from truth," I replied.

"Do you know how to use these magic sticks?" he continued.

"Yes."

"Are you then a magician?"

"No, anyone can do it if he has the things to go with them," I explained. "I mean some black powder made for the purpose and some round, hard balls."

"*Hoh, do-gehs' oh-yah'-neh.* Truly fine. Already I have everything. One of my scouts brought me a magic stick, a horn full of black powder and some little hard balls in a shoulder pouch. Will you teach me to use them?"

I hesitated. "How do I know that you will not turn this weapon against my kinsmen among the English and the Lenapes?"

"You will understand after I have told you a few things," he said. "I suppose you know that the Five Nations have been attacked several times already by people from across the Great Water."

"None of our English people have done so, or I would have heard of it," I said.

"These people came upon us from the North," he explained.

I thought for a moment. "Oh, you must mean the French!"

"Are the '*P-Klensh*' different from the *Yen'-gees?*" he demanded.

"Yes! They talk a different language, too."

"They struck at the Standing Stone People (Oneidas) only last year," he continued, "and our warriors drove them back, in spite of their magic sticks. But they will come again. I thought at first you were one of them. Now my scouts bring word from the South that there are many *Yen'-gees* already on these shores and more coming all the time, well armed with magic weapons. Should the *Yen'-gees* attack us from the South and the *P-Klensh* from the North, and both with magic thunder sticks, the Five Nations would be in danger.

"The *P-Klensh* have already shown themselves to be hostile, so our best plan is to make friends with the *Yen'-gees* and in this you shall advise me. As for the Lenapes, they have agreed to become peacemakers instead of warriors. If they keep their promise, my weapons will not be turned against them.

"Now, listen; I have freed your brother, Little-Bear. In return you must promise me two things."

"What are they?"

"When you return to *Gah-nah-dah-go'-nah* you will be my adviser concerning our dealings with the *Yen'-gees;* and second, you will show me how to work my magic thunder stick."

"I am thankful for the release of Little-Bear, and when I return, if nothing happens to prevent, I agree to do these things," I promised, but I purposely did not name the time of my return.

"*Nyoh!*" he exclaimed. "So be it! Now one more thing. I want you to know that Big-Nose went beyond his orders in testing you!"

"You mean when the stones fell on me? Yes? Then how about the rattlesnakes? If that was a test, it was a dangerous one, also."

"Not as dangerous as it appeared. If you had looked into the mouths of the snakes you would have seen that the poison teeth had been pulled out. And there is one thing more I must tell you; Big-Nose informs me that he will no longer obey all my orders!"

"What do you mean?"

"He says if I tell him again to bother you or your women in any way he will refuse—you had a chance to kill him and a good excuse for doing it. Instead, you gave him food for his journey home!"

Going back to the council house, we found my faithful companions, with Little-Bear, waiting at the door. They looked greatly relieved when I returned unharmed with Tadoda'ho.

Next day our two brave women still had nothing to say.

"If they don't want to talk," I thought, "it is not for me to force them." Nevertheless it worried me. What was wrong?

They were lying in their bunks that evening while I was gazing gloomily into the fire, when Many-Tongues pranced into the cabin.

"Wake up, you sleepy folks!" he piped. "I have some news for you."

"What is it?" I demanded. Among-the-Blossoms sat up. I noticed her eyes were wet.

"Tadoda'ho and his party are leaving for Onondaga early tomorrow morning," he announced. "And I am going with them."

"Don't do that," Among-the-Blossoms urged, "stay with us until—until the end."

"I don't know what you mean," he said, "but my work is done. Big-Turtle can talk sweet to his girls now, without help from me; and you all know enough Seneca to get along. Besides, this is a good chance for me to travel with a party. Nobody knows when you slow corn-worms will be back; maybe not until you are old and feeble. Now I must get my things ready."

We saw him off the next morning at dawn. As the party rounded a bend in the trail he waved to us and shouted: "Two of you should get married. Guess which!"

Among-the-Blossoms looked up at me; she was ready to weep, why I could not guess. I put my arm around her, tried to comfort her. There was no need now to fight off my feelings toward her. But she pulled away after a moment or two and went back into the cabin, and Mother followed.

Later in the morning Hiawatha asked me what had passed between Tadoda'ho and myself, and I told him everything.

"Tadoda'ho may have really thought you were an enemy spy when he intended to put you to death by torture; then you were adopted into the tribe and he did not dare. The first tricks he had played upon you were, I think, not tests, but just to torment you for having been the cause of his shame before the people. Later, when he discovered who you were, and that you had courage and a good head, he decided he might use you. And then he really tried to test you—especially that night in the council house.

"Tadoda'ho thinks of only two things; his own glory, and the welfare of the Five Nations. We forgive the first on account of the second."

Later Hiawatha and his companions left to complete their last tour of the villages of the Five Nations they had united into a powerful League.

Before they started I ventured to ask Jigon'sasay, the Mother of Nations, what was in the bundle on her back.

"It is a sacred smoking pipe," the old chieftainess said, swinging the bundle around and caressing it tenderly, "that was sent to me by a Western tribe. When it is smoked, all present must listen to words of peace."

Then I addressed the three of them.

"I am little more than a boy," I said, "I know it is very bold of me, but I wish to tell you what is in my heart."

"Go ahead and speak," rumbled Deganawi'da.

"In planting the Great Tree of Peace," I said, "you three have done a most wonderful thing. I am proud and thankful I had the chance to know you."

"We hope that the Tree will continue to grow after we are gone," said Hiawatha. "And that all the nations will some day gather beneath its branches," he paused for a moment, looking me in the eye. "Even those on the other side of the Great Water," he concluded.

I watched them as they disappeared down the valley with their guards and bearers.

The night before Little-Bear was to leave, the friends he had made among the Big Mountain People gave him a farewell party: they called it "pushing off his canoe."

Naturally I attended, and as I sat, watching the dancers, thoughts were pressing upon me—thoughts of my Iroquois friends, of .Little-Bear, of my own future. I had been letting things slide, but now I must make a decision.

Should I, could I, go back to Lenape Land with Little-Bear? Absolutely not. Even if it were not for Among-the-Blossoms, my precious adopted mother, and my promise to Tadoda'ho, what would I do in Turtle-Town? Help Little-Bear hunt food to feed his family, perhaps, and that is about all. And then that danger of family trouble which I especially .dreaded. I had no desire to go on to Jamestown with my uncle there. At least until I was sure my parents had come back from England—and it was far too soon.

If on the other hand I returned to Onondaga land, I would keep my promise to Tadoda'ho, and as his adviser, I would play a useful part, if a small one, in managing the League of the Iroquois, which I admired so much; and in keeping peace between the League and my English kinsmen; both really worthwhile.

But more important were my dear Among-the-Blossoms and Carrying-Woman who together had saved my life—were ready any time, as I had seen, to risk theirs for mine. I thought over all that had happened.

Everything started with Among-the-Blossoms, when she decided to save me; without her I would be dead to-day and Little-Bear still a captive. Yet she could not have saved me without the help of Carrying-Woman; and even these two could not have made this trip with me, without Many-Tongues. Without my being here, Hiawatha could not have found Little-Bear for me; and unless he had done this, Tadoda'ho could not have arranged his release.

Yes, there had been many helpers, but Among-the-Blossoms was the foundation of everything. I looked at her, that wonderful girl, where she sat on the woman's side of the council house, her slim form clad in the embroidered dress I had earned for her among the Cayugas. Her eyes were turned down, toward the floor, not at the dancers, and her arms were moving restlessly. She must be thinking of something serious. My heart warmed strongly toward her.

As I watched, she rose and left the council house. I slipped out also; yes, there she was, plain in the moonlight, crossing the public square in the direction of the cabin where we were quartered.

I followed; but to my shocked surprise; Carrying-Woman blocked the way when I tried to enter the doorway.

"Where is Among-the-Blossoms?" I demanded.

"She does not want to see you!"

I pushed past. In the flickering firelight I could see the girl, clad in all her finery, lying face-down on her bunk. Her shoulders were heaving. I called her name. No answer.

I laid my hand on her shoulder. She whispered something that sounded like *"Sah-dend'-yah!"* which means "Go away!"

"What is the matter with her?" I asked Carrying-Woman.

"She can't stand it!"

"Can't stand what?"

"That you are going away tomorrow, back to Lenape land with your brother."

"Who says I am going?"

"Why, everybody knows it."

"Then everybody knows wrong!"

As I spoke, Among-the-Blossoms sat up. Her face was streaked with tears. "You mean," she said, "you are not going away?"

"I am not going away!"

The next minute she was in my arms. I held her tight, kissed her again and again. No doubt about it, we belonged to each other.

Finally Mother said "I think you two had better get married even before we start back to Onondaga land. But right now don't you think we had better help 'push off' Little-Bear's 'canoe'?"

A few minutes later we entered the council house. The party was over, and his friends were filing by to shake his hand and wish him a safe journey. I could not catch the Seneca words they used, but Carrying-Woman whispered to me the Onondaga version—"I hope the ca-

noe that carries you will escape the perils of stormy waters, of rapids, rocks and snags, and will bear you home
in safety!" Yet everybody knew that he had no canoe, but
expected to travel on foot.

We joined the line, I leading. When Little-Bear
heard the same wish from me, translated into Lenape,
his jaw dropped.

"What's this?" he demanded. "Aren't you coming
home with me tomorrow?"

"No, Elder Brother," I told him. "Not this time.
You see, I promised to do some things for Tadoda'ho in
return for your release, and must go back to the Onondaga country. Tell Bowl-Woman I still love her, and not
to worry, because now I have an Iroquois mother too."
I took hold of Carrying-Woman's arm. "Here she is. She
helped save my life and will watch over me."

"Who did you say this girl is?" Little-Bear demanded, looking at Among-the-Blossoms.

"What did he say?" she asked. I interpreted. She
shot me a mischievous glance.

"Tell him 'Sister' would be a good name for him to
call me the way things look now!"

Next morning we watched them disappear down the
trail; Moonhakee, whining, started to follow, but I called
him back. Then by common impulse we returned to the
cabin and seated ourselves on the platform. The two
women, also the dog, looked at me expectantly. The time
had come!

"Dear One," I said to Among-the-Blossoms. "Would
you rather get your new name now, or after we go back
to Onondaga land?"

"What new name?" she demanded. "Don't you like the one I have now?"

"Truly," I replied. "But in the land where I was born, across the Great Water, every person carries two names, their own and their family name. When a woman marries she keeps her own, but takes her husband's family name. Then she is often called by his full name, with the word 'Mrs.' before it, which means 'Wife of.' I am known among the *Yen'-gees* as Dickon, but my real name is Richard and my family name Sherwood; so my wife will be called Mrs. Richard Sherwood."

"How do you say it?" she asked. "Meesus Wih-chad Shuh-wood?" She hung her head and whispered. "I would like that new name very soon!"

I don't know how it was managed, but through Mother's efforts the village chiefs and some of the others got together—probably because they felt that we were friends of Hiawatha—and arranged for the great event that very afternoon.

Weddings are usually held in a private cabin or in the long-house of the bride's clan; but the chiefs decided that ours should be in the council house, at the very spot where Among-the-Blossoms risked her life to protect me from Tadoda'ho's war club.

When all was ready, Mother called me, gave me instructions, and, as in a dream, we walked into the council house. A new mat had been spread at the spot, and on one end of this I was told to kneel, facing the center. I noticed then that quite a crowd had gathered to watch, including some of the chiefs. Mother took her stand behind me, and Moonhakee seated himself nearby.

Now Among-the-Blossoms walked sedately in, wearing the finery I had won for her among the Cayugas—she looked really beautiful. She was carrying a polished wooden bowl, which she set down upon the mat in front of me, and knelt, facing me, on the other side of it.

There was a breathless silence—and then I managed to say, as I had been instructed, *"Oh-neh' wa-ong-nee-nyah'-kay!"* and she repeated the words. They mean "Now we two marry!"

In the bowl were two small carved wooden spoons—also some food, *oh-no'-kwa*. She took a spoon, filled it, and slowly and daintily placed the contents in my mouth. I chewed and swallowed, and then, with the other spoon, did the same for her; then we ate the rest of the *oh-no'-kwa*. At this a woman stepped up bearing a basket full of steaming little cornhusk bundles with an appetizing smell.

Among-the-Blossoms took one, unwrapped it; inside were two smaller ones, also wrapped in husks, each containing a little round corncake. She put one cake in my mouth, the other in her own. They tasted very good, being made with tree sugar.

Now my bride added something of her own to the ceremony. She asked, "Am I now Meesus Wih-chad Shuh-wood?" Of course I answered "You are now Mrs. Richard Sherwood!" And Mother announced in a loud voice, "Now these two are married!"

I only wish I had had a wedding ring to put on my bride's finger, to look at now and then to reassure myself that she was really my wife. Eventually I was able to get one for her, but that was years later.

We rose to our feet and my new wife passed around

the basket, distributing the "bride's bread" as long as it lasted. Then we stood together while the crowd filed by to wish us well. We could not understand just what they said, unless they spoke in Onondaga, which some of them did.

Hardly had the last one gone out the door when we were in each other's arms. "My husband!"—"My wife!" After a while my bride said "One thing I'd like to ask, now that I am your wife. I would like to call you by your *Yen'-gees* name, Dickon, instead of Big-Turtle. Is that all right with you?"

"Truly it is," I told her, and kissed her again.

"And could you call me by a short *Yen'-gees* name?"

I thought for a moment. "I can call you Blossoms," I said. "That is a *Yen'-gees* word for part of your Onondaga name."

"I would like that," she said, and raised her lips for another kiss.

Just then Mother touched me on the shoulder.

"Night has come," she said. "And the fires in this building are about burned out. Why don't you old married folks go to the cabin? It is all yours. Moonhakee and I will spend the night in the Turtle Clan long-house."

The cabin faced east, and the next morning my wife and I stood in the doorway, watching the sunrise. We agreed that it was the most beautiful we had ever seen!

IROQUOIS LANGUAGE
(mostly Onondaga)

Ah-geh'	Alas
Ah-gwas'	Very
Ah-kee'	Alas, ouch
Ah-tah'-gwah	Moccasin
Ah-wen-hah-gon'-wa	Among-the-Blossoms
Day-gah-nah-wee'-dah	Deganawida. Two-Streams-Flowing-Together
Day-hat-kah'-dons	Looks-Both-Ways
Day-weh-nee-do'-geh	Between-Two-Moons
Deh-yo-hay'-yo-go	Floating-Rushes, a Cayuga village
Do-gehs'	Truly
Dus'-hah-wah	Give me
Dus-nay-gah'-hwah	Give me water
Ees	You
Gah'-jee	Come here
Gah-nah-dah-go'-nah	Big-Town
Ga-nun-dah'-gway	Town-Selected, a Seneca village

Ga-yah'-jee	Name
Go-dah-eh-gehs'-geh	Smelly-Mud, a Seneca village
Goon-wah-hah'-wee	Carrying-Woman
Go'-weh	Messenger's call
Gweh!	Exclamation, similar to "gee!"
Hah-doo'-wee	Mask Spirit
Hah-nya-denh-goh'-nah	Big-Turtle
Haht-deh-gah-yeh'-ee	That's enough!
Hah-yah-went'-ha	Hiawatha. He-Makes-Rivers
Hau	An exclamation
Hee-yah'	No, not
Hee-yah'-tah-gah-yah'-ee	Nothing at all
Hee-yah'-teh	Not
Ho-dee-gon-sa-sonh'-onh	Company of Faces
Hoht-nen'-geh	What's this?
Ho-nah-sah-gah'-deh	Many-Tongues
Ho-nyuh-sah-go'-nah	Big-Nose
Ik-sa-goh'-nah	Maiden
Jee-gah-eh-heh'-wa	Stone-Roller goblin
Jee-gon'-sah-say	Jigonsasay, called "Peace Woman"
Jon-nes'-see-yoh	Genessee
Ka-ha-ma'-kun	Parched corn (Lenape)
Nay-gah-nay-gah'-ah	Little Water Society, Little Water medicine
Nay'-toh	Here
Nee-yah-weh'-ha	Thanks
Neh	The
Nyoh	So be it
Oh-nay'-gah-nos	Water
Oh-neh'	Now
Oh'-nih	Also
Oh-no'-kwa	Hominy
Oht-goh'-eh	Wampum
Oh-wah'-jee-yah	Family group

Oh-yah'-neh	Good
Oh-yen'-gwah	Tobacco
O-nen'-ha o-non'-deh	Ground parched corn
O-nen-hon'-deh	Ground parched corn
On'-gweh On'-weh	Person-Real (Iroquois)
On-on-da-geh-hay'-nah	Hill People (Onondagas)
Ot-chee'	Horrors!
Ot'-gon	Evil
Sah-dend'-yah	Go away
Sahd-yenh'	Sit down
Saht-gaht'-to	Look
Sah'-yenh-geh	Have you?
Sen-dah-no'-gehs	You lie
Sgon-see'-geh	Thy face
Shah-go-jo-weh'-go-wa	Mask Spirit (Seneca)
Shee'-kee	Fine! (Lenape)
Skeh-nong'-hah	Slowly
Sup-pan	Hominy (Lenape)
Sway'-geh	A Cayuga river
Thak-gway'-nee-ah	Am able
Ut'-kee	Dirty
Wahk'-yenh	I have
Wah-nee'-shih	Thank you (Lenape)
Wah-pay-wee'-pit	White-Tooth (Lenape)
Wa-ong-nee-nyah'-kay	We two marry
Yen'-gees	English